A PIG CALLED FRANCIS BACON

A PIG CALLED
FRANCIS BACON

Stephen Measday

Mammoth

First published in Australia 1996
by Reed for Kids
First published in Great Britain 1996
by Mammoth, an imprint of Reed International Books Ltd
Michelin House, 81 Fulham Road, London SW3 6RB
and Auckland and Melbourne

Copyright © Stephen Measday 1996

The moral rights of the author have been asserted.

ISBN 0 7497 3151 6

A CIP catalogue record for this title
is available from the British Library

Printed and bound in Great Britain
by Cox & Wyman Ltd, Reading, Berkshire

To Rene Measday
the storyteller in our tribe
with love

Contents

1

THE WIDE WORLD

Francis Bacon was bored from looking at the four white walls around him and, to his left and right, at the steel pens that held a dozen other pigs.

'Snuff ... slurrp ... thrurrp!'

The air was alive with the sounds of grunting and chewing, as the pigs ate their second meal of the day – a mixture that never changed – wheat and barley, vitamins, minerals and fresh fruit and vegetables.

Francis had finished his already. Unlike the others, he didn't think about food much; it didn't interest him. His mind was on other things.

It annoyed Francis that there were no

windows in the building – only lights on the ceiling in long tubes. And the air was circulated by machines that hummed all the time and kept the temperature the same.

Sometimes, when the other pigs were quiet or sleeping, Francis thought he heard things happening outside – the sound of a bird call, a car engine revving, or a strong wind whipping through the trees.

But he was never sure if the sounds were real or just his imagination.

Francis was also puzzled. He noticed that every few weeks, one or two fully grown pigs would be taken from their pens – and they never came back. The pigs were replaced by a couple of piglets, but where they had gone was a mystery.

With plenty of time on his trotters, two big questions really stuck in his mind. Would he also have to leave one day? And what was it like outside, in that world he couldn't see?

Francis was itching to find out.

2

GIRT BY SEA

The long green valley that lay between the mountains in the west and the hills in the east was pig-growing country. And the local farmers were proud of it.

Lucy Russo always laughed when she saw the town's roadside sign, which pictured a big pink pig and the friendly greeting, WELCOME! MAKIN VALLEY IS BACON VALLEY.

'If we're not makin' bacon, we're not makin' money,' Uncle Reg said as they drove down the highway.

'And it's all talk, if we're not growin' pork,' Lucy replied.

This routine was one Lucy and her uncle

repeated whenever she came up from the city to stay with him and her aunt on their farm. This holidays, Lucy's mum and dad were in Italy visiting her grandparents, but Lucy didn't mind being left behind. This was the best couple of weeks of the year, when Uncle Reg got his prize pigs ready for the Easter Show.

Reg flicked the ute's indicator and the car turned onto the freshly graded dirt road leading to the house.

'I've put up a new sign at our place too,' Reg said with a grin that lit up his suntanned face.

'You mean you've finally found a name for the farm?'

'Yep.'

Lucy thought about all the fun they'd had thinking of interesting names. On past holidays, they'd fallen about hilariously as they came up with names like Pork Park, Crackle Creek and Grazelands.

Reg pointed to the main gate and Lucy looked at the sign overhead – GIRT BY SEA STUD.

'Like in the national anthem,' she said.

'Australians all let us rejoice ...' Reg began.

Lucy joined in. 'For we are young and free.

We've golden soil and wealth for toil. Our home is girt by sea ...'

'You got it.'

'We're a long way from the sea,' Lucy said, not too seriously.

'Yeah, but I figure the whole country's surrounded by ocean, and I was looking for a real Aussie name. At this year's Show, my pigs will be from the Girt By Sea Stud.'

'Can't get more Aussie than that,' Lucy agreed. 'I like it.'

Aunt Vittoria was waiting in front of the house and waved as the ute came to a stop. Lucy was out of the car in a flash and Vittoria hugged her tight and swung her off the ground.

'Oh, Lucinda, I'll have to stop doing this! You're heavier than a bag of wheat,' Vittoria groaned, putting her niece down. Lucy was tall for twelve and dark-haired like Vittoria, and her mother, Claudia.

A car horn tooted behind them and a late-model white sedan drove slowly up the track. The fair-haired woman at the wheel nodded at Reg as she went by.

Lucy's eyes followed the car. 'Who's that?'

'Dr Price,' Vittoria replied. 'Dr Amanda Price.'

Before Lucy could ask why a doctor was here, she saw where the car was heading – towards a large white building in the paddock behind the house. It was surrounded by a high-security wire fence, and as Dr Price approached it, she put her right arm out of the car window and pointed a remote control at the main gate. It silently swung open and the car went inside.

Lucy looked curiously at Vittoria. 'And what's that? When did you build that?'

Vittoria took her niece's hand. 'Come inside and unpack. Then we'll tell you everything.'

3
GENIUS GENES

'It's pretty simple, Lucy,' Reg explained. 'Late last year, just after you were here, these blokes turned up from some scientific outfit –'

'The Genius Genes Corporation,' Vittoria chipped in.

'Yeah, that's right; this mob of geniuses turned up.' Reg's mouth creased in a mischievous smile.

'Maybe genii is more than one?' Lucy suggested.

'Nah, they come out of brass lamps and give you three wishes.'

Lucy and Reg chuckled.

'Reg, you were saying ...' Vittoria knew that if

she didn't keep them on the subject, they'd go off all over the place.

'Yeah, these people reckoned they wanted to build this scientific type of pig shed out the back,' Reg continued. 'And they wanted me to supply them with some of my prime breeding pigs.'

'And you said OK.'

'Sure, I produce good pigs. And it's tough on the land. You make dough where you can these days.'

Lucy noticed the little wrinkles of worry around Uncle Reg's eyes and on his forehead. He and Aunt Vittoria worked long hours and the chance to make some extra money must have been welcome. 'But what do they do in there?' she asked.

'They work in some new area of science,' Vittoria said. 'I think they call it biogenetics, you know, genetic engineering. It's all to do with breeding new types of animals.'

'Wow! Like in *Jurassic Park*?' Lucy pictured hundreds of lizardy animals with big sharp teeth hopping around inside the building.

'Except they're pigs, not dinosaurs,' Vittoria added.

'Who cares if they're one-legged ducks?' Reg

shrugged. 'They buy my pigs and they buy my feed. Doesn't worry me what they're doing. Another sandwich anyone?'

Lucy took one from the plate and thought things over.

'Oh, Lucy,' Vittoria said. 'Bob Jones rang from Waringa. Do you want to go over and see Sara and Andy? They're on holidays too.'

'Maybe later.' Sara and Andy were friends who lived on a farm nearby, but boarded in the city. Lucy figured she could see them any time. At the moment she was more curious about things that were happening here.

It was time for a look around.

Lucy stood near the front gate, squinting at the bright sunlight bouncing off the new white building. It was so different to Uncle Reg's pig shed, it was hard to imagine it was a piggery at all.

Uncle Reg's shed, which held about three hundred boars, sows and piglets, was about half a kilometre from the house, in the opposite direction. It was open to the air on three sides and an underground bore supplied it with fresh water. Although it wasn't too scientific, Uncle Reg did have some up-to-date equipment. There was an automatic machine to feed the pigs, and a special program on his computer allowed him to choose the best pigs for cross-breeding.

'You have to use a bit of science these days to keep up the quality of the herd,' Uncle Reg had often told her. 'But not too much or you get confused.'

Lucy liked his shed – it was noisy and a bit smelly. She was sure the pigs were happy and contented. She could spend the whole day there and never get bored.

However, Lucy had her doubts about this new building. It was weird.

For a start, the site had been chosen carefully; it was well away from the main road, and most of the structure was hidden behind a screen of tall gum trees and wattle bushes. And the sign on the gate didn't exactly throw out the welcome mat:

> **GENIUS GENES CORPORATION**
> **NO ENTRY!**
> **TRESPASSERS PROSECUTED**
> **BE WARNED!**

Lucy strolled around the high, wire fence. The building was about fifty metres long and about twenty wide, with only one small window at one end. The only sound came from the air-conditioning unit on the roof. What did the pigs do in there? Lucy wondered.

She felt uneasy. One thing she liked about coming to the farm was that nothing really changed. You got up early and there were chores to do. Afterwards, you could mess around by the creek, visit the pigs or take trips into town with Uncle Reg. And Aunt Vittoria cooked lots of lasagne and spaghetti and you could eat as much as you liked. Now, the farm has a secret, Lucy thought, there's a place I can't go. It made her angry.

'Oh, h-hi!' Lucy said, surprised. She was back at the entrance to the building and had nearly bumped into Dr Price.

'Hullo,' Amanda said, closing a smaller gate alongside the main entrance. 'I was just coming over to see your uncle. You're Lucy, aren't you?'

'Yeah, Lucy Russo. Vittoria's my aunt.'

'I know. She told me you were coming to visit.'

Amanda moved towards the house and Lucy

followed. 'Do you mind me asking what sort of doctor you are?'

'Not at all. I'm a type of chemist. A doctor of biochemistry and biological science.'

That sounded very impressive, but Lucy needed to know more. 'You don't fix up people then?'

'No, I'm not that sort of doctor.'

'Can I ask you something else?'

'Ask away.'

'What do you do in there?' Lucy glanced back at the building.

'We breed pigs. Like your uncle does.' Amanda ended the conversation with a tight smile and walked on ahead. 'See you later.'

'Bye, Dr Price.'

Amanda knocked on the front door of the farmhouse and Uncle Reg invited her inside.

I've just got the shove-off, Lucy decided; a mind-your-own-business from Dr Price. But why was she so secretive about her work?

More than ever, Lucy wanted to know what went on behind those walls.

4

HOW NOW PINK SOW

Lucy yawned and wondered when she'd ever get to bed and get some sleep.

'That's the last one,' Reg said cheerfully. 'Look, Luce, a terrific litter. Nine of them.'

From the railing, Lucy looked down into the pen where the farm's prize sow, Matilda, had just given birth to a new litter of piglets. As often happened, Reg had stayed overnight, in case the sow got into any difficulties. Lucy had kept him company and, fortunately, all had gone well.

'Hey, we might take this lot to the Show,' Reg beamed. 'I'll enter a sow and litter. What do you reckon?'

Lucy was fully awake now and smiled at the piglets squirming around Matilda's stomach, desperately wriggling in for the first feed of their lives. 'I think it's a good idea. They look great. And Matilda loves the Show.' At last year's Show, Matilda had won the Champion Sow's blue ribbon and had strutted proudly around the ring like she was born to win.

'Well, she could easily be champion again.' Reg gave Matilda a pat on the head and a rub around the ears. 'Come on, we'll let her rest. These little guys will have to feed every hour, twenty-four hours a day. Better leave her to it.'

'Can we have breakfast now? I'm starving.'

Lucy tried not to think of bacon and eggs. In the city it didn't seem to matter, but when she got to know all the pigs at the farm again, she didn't have the stomach for it. This morning, cereal and orange juice would be fine.

'After we mix up the day's feed for Dr Price's pigs,' Reg said. 'Won't take long.'

Reg and Lucy sat on the tractor while Amanda opened the main gate in front of the white building. Reg slipped the tractor into gear and towed the feed bin up to the roll-a-door entrance.

'Won't be a sec.' Amanda punched some numbers on a small electronic pad by the door. With a whirring noise, the door rolled up to reveal a loading bay. Once inside, Reg climbed down from the tractor and pushed a lever. The feed bin tipped its contents into a stainless steel hopper. From here, the food went through a pipe into the mysterious interior of the building.

Now she had the chance, Lucy looked around carefully. Apart from the roll-a-door, the only other way to get inside was through a door at the far end of the loading bay. However, it appeared to be securely locked. That must lead into the main part of the building, Lucy decided.

'Have to deliver the feed here every day,' Reg explained. 'The porkers get it fresh and they get plenty of it.'

'Lucy, would you like to have a look around?' Amanda said.

'What? In there?' Lucy pointed to the locked door.

'Sure. In fact, while you're on holidays, you

might be able to help me with the feeding. I've discussed it with Reg.'

'Dr Price goes away at the weekends,' Reg said. 'Normally, I do it, but I'm pretty busy getting ready for the Show. I told the doc you were a hard worker. Is that OK with you?'

'Yeah, sure,' Lucy agreed. 'I'd like to help.'

'Good. You better come with me.' Amanda unlocked the door and stepped inside.

Lucy couldn't believe her luck. This was turning out better than she could have planned.

5

BEHIND CLOSED DOORS

The first thing Lucy noticed was how clean and quiet it was – like a hospital. The room had pale-green tiled walls, and was full of pig-feeding machinery.

The pipe from the hopper came through the wall and ended above a long conveyor belt. Two large bins containing some kind of powder stood nearby. A few metres away, a glass sliding door and a wide observation window revealed a much bigger room. Lucy saw some pens and could hear faint pig noises.

'The first thing you have to do, is put on these.' Amanda showed her a rack of blue overalls hanging by the door. 'You're probably about the same size as our cleaner. Try hers on. They go over your jeans and t-shirt.'

Lucy watched Amanda slip into the protective clothing and then did the same.

'And these too.' Amanda handed her a pair of rubber boots and a hair net in a plastic pack. 'We have to keep things pretty clean. Because of the sort of work we do.'

Lucy desperately wanted to ask what kind of work, but decided to get the gear on first. The boots were a bit big and the overalls were crisp and starched. She felt like an astronaut about to walk on the moon.

'This way, Lucy.' Amanda pulled on her hair net and stepped into a shallow metal tray that stank of disinfectant.

'What's that for?' asked Lucy, as she struggled to get all her hair into the net.

'It stops you from bringing germs in on your boots – walk through it every time you come in. OK, I'll show you how we mix the feed.'

Amanda stopped at a control panel, pressed a green button and the conveyor started to move. She pressed a yellow button and a stream of wheat, barley, fruit and vegetables poured onto the belt – the mixture that Reg made up every day and delivered to the loading bay.

'Just add half a dozen scoops from these two bins as the stuff goes by,' said Amanda, demonstrating. 'It's vitamins and a few other things to keep the pigs healthy and make them grow. Any problems so far?'

'Looks pretty easy.'

'Then it moves along to this mixer.' Amanda touched a large square bin that whirred like a giant washing machine on spin dry. 'And from there, it goes inside.'

Lucy joined Amanda at the window and looked into the biggest part of the building. There were four rows of pig pens, with a passageway between each row. She counted twenty-four pens, half of which were occupied – by the pinkest, cleanest pigs she'd ever seen.

'From here,' Amanda pointed at the mixer, 'the food goes to each of the pens. Look.' She pressed a red button, the mixer vibrated and a vacuuming kind of sound came from the four pipes fixed into the top of the machine. Through the window, Lucy saw the food drop from a narrower pipe fixed above each pig's trough. With a clatter of trotters and excited grunts, the pigs got stuck into their breakfast.

'It's a bit like Uncle Reg's feeding system. But much more ...' Lucy tried to find the right word.

'Sophisticated,' Amanda suggested. 'Each pig gets exactly the right amount of food for its rate of growth and body weight. The in-house computer system controls everything else as well – like keeping the temperature constant at twenty-two degrees.'

'What about water?'

'There's a tap in each pen, which the pigs have been taught to operate.'

'The pigs do it?'

'Sure, they're pretty intelligent animals. Genetically, they're ninety-seven percent the same as humans, you know. Though some are more intelligent than others,' Dr Price added.

'They're all cross-bred,' Lucy observed. 'Landrace Large White Cross.'

'Yes, they're the best.'

Lucy couldn't resist asking, 'For what, Dr Price?'

'Don't ask too many questions,' she replied, firmly but pleasantly. 'A lot happens here that isn't easy to explain.'

At that moment, Lucy knew exactly what the

doctor meant. She noticed one pig near the end of the second row. He was a little bigger than the others and there was something strange about his pen – it had furniture in it. A bookstand and a tall desk lamp stood in one corner. And that wasn't all.

Lucy blinked and looked again to make sure she wasn't seeing things. The pig was staring at a book on the stand. His long pink tongue flicked out and turned the page. As *if he was reading*. Or was this a trick, she thought, like teaching them to turn on taps?

'Dr Price, that pig over –'

'No more questions please, Lucy,' said Amanda, walking away. 'I'll show you the combination for the outside door so you'll be able to get in. And, can I ask a favour?'

'Sure.'

'Don't go in there.' She indicated the pig pen area. 'Just feed them and leave. And toss your overalls in the laundry basket when you go. You need to put on a fresh pair every time you come. OK?'

'Fine.'

As she left, Lucy glanced back at the pig. His tongue poked out and turned another page.

Surely, this one had to be more intelligent than the others. And how would Dr Price ever explain that?

'You sure you don't want an egg?' Vittoria said. 'There's two, I'm only having one.'

Lucy spread a thick layer of crunchy peanut butter on her toast as Vittoria fished a boiled egg from the saucepan on the stove. 'No, toast's all right. So, where does Dr Price go at the weekends?'

Uncle Reg had gone into Makinville to get some veterinary supplies and to hire a truck to take the pigs to the Show in a week's time, and Lucy had seized the opportunity to quiz her aunt about Dr Price.

'Look, I don't know a lot about her,' Vittoria confessed. 'From what she's said, I gather her husband is a neurosurgeon at one of the major city hospitals.'

'What's a neuro ... thingo?'

'He operates on people's heads – their brains.'

'I've seen that on TV,' Lucy said. 'Don't they saw people's heads open and take a geek inside?'

'Yes, something like that.' Vittoria smiled at

her niece. She'd always been one of those kids who never stopped asking 'why?' It annoyed her mother, but here on the farm it seemed quite natural. 'All I know is that they have a house in the city and she goes back every weekend to spend some time with her husband. And their son.'

'She's got a kid?'

'Yes. His name's Henry. But she doesn't talk about him much.'

'Why?'

'There's something wrong with him. He spends a lot of time in hospital. Cancer, I think.'

'Oh, right.' Now Lucy felt guilty. 'Sorry, I was just curious about her.'

'That's OK,' Vittoria replied. 'Anything else and you'll have to ask Dr Price herself.'

Fat chance of that, Lucy thought. If I ask any more questions, Dr Price might stop me going into the building. And with a sick son, and all those pigs, she probably has enough to worry about.

'Has Uncle Reg ever had a pig that could read books?' As soon as she said it, Lucy knew it sounded really stupid.

Vittoria laughed loudly. 'A lot of his pigs are

smart. But not that smart. Why do you want to know?'

'Oh, no reason.' Lucy wanted to change the subject quickly. 'I just wondered, that's all.' She pushed her chair back from the table and left the room. 'See ya.'

6
FACE TO FACE

The sight of an unfamiliar human being would have made most pigs nervous. But not Francis.

Pigs are creatures of habit; they take a long time to get used to their handlers, and they hate it whenever anyone new turns up. Francis felt differently: any change of routine was a stroke of luck to be welcomed and enjoyed.

This morning, it had taken him only a few seconds to notice that someone new was preparing the food. He placed his front trotters on the bottom rail of the pen, lifted himself up, and looked towards the big window.

She's younger and slimmer than Dr Price and not as tall as that dark-haired man who comes in occasionally, Francis quietly observed. And for some reason, she keeps looking at me too.

With a noisy burst of whooshes and rattles, the food dropped into the dozen troughs around the room and the pigs began their meal.

Francis had forgotten to eat the previous night because he'd been reading *Oliver Twist* by Charles Dickens, and he'd found the story of the lonely orphan boy too interesting to interrupt. As any uneaten food was automatically flushed away after mealtimes, Francis had experienced a long and hungry wait until breakfast.

He sniffed around the trough and sunk his teeth into a tasty Granny Smith apple. He enjoyed the crunch of the fruit and the burst of sweet juice in his mouth. Then he saw the girl at the window again.

She gave him a friendly smile.

There's no doubt she's communicating with me, Francis thought. Perhaps this was how friendships started? Judging from what he'd read, making – and losing – friends was a major part of life, and this might be an ideal opportunity to experience it himself.

Francis looked towards the window, crinkled up his lips and twitched his nose.

That pig smiled back at me, Lucy realised. Unless she was mistaken, that flash of choppers and wriggling nose was as close to a smile as a pig could get. She was immediately faced with a huge dilemma: what was she going to do?

Dr Price wasn't due back for another twenty-four hours – till Sunday afternoon. Before then, Lucy had to feed the pigs five more times. How was she going to stop watching and thinking about that pig? It was impossible. The obvious thing to do is forget him, she told herself. I'll take off my overalls and boots, put my hair net in the bin and leave.

But, instead, she moved closer to the glass door. Her hand hovered over the metal button that opened and shut it. A few metres away, some of the pigs snuffled in their troughs, taking no notice of her.

Lucy slapped the button with the palm of her hand and the door glided into a recess in the wall. She stepped inside and felt the air-conditioned warmth creep along her arms and down her neck. Cautiously, she walked past the first pen, where a piglet was eating greedily. She entered the second row and passed the first three pens, numbered B1, B2 and B3. A round, red sticker had been stuck next to the label B2. Lucy leaned over the rail and watched as the sow, about six months old, licked out her trough. Wondering what the red sticker meant, Lucy moved on.

She glanced at B4, then stopped before the second-last pen in the row. Instead of being labelled B5, the pen had the name FRANCIS written on it in large black letters. The pig raised his eyebrows in a curious expression.

Without thinking, Lucy blurted, 'Hullo, piggy. How are you?'

The pig chewed his food thoroughly, swallowed and his mouth opened. 'Hi, dag. Thanks for getting it on and coming on down. You cool?'

'I ... I ...' Lucy panicked and ran back down the row. She fled through the door and it whooshed shut behind her.

Francis was dumbstruck. Why had the girl run off like that? Dr Price had given him a few teenage novels to read lately and he had studied the modern language carefully. However, it hadn't worked on this younger person at all. Did all friendships start as badly as this? he wondered. Grumpily, he flopped onto the floor and stared at the ceiling.

Just as they had a hundred times before, his eyes roved over the fluorescent lights, the endless lines of electrical wiring and the wide sections of whiteboard that insulated the building from the weather outside. He knew every crack and every mark on the ceiling.

Sometimes, he made the lines and cracks into the maps of imaginary countries. He called one of these countries Suidae (after the name that zoologists gave to the pig family). In Suidae, Francis was President and could go anywhere he liked. By train, car, bus or by plane. He was allowed to camp out in a tent and sit around a fire and stare at the moon and stars. He could talk to all sorts of fascinating people and meet exotic animals, like lemurs, elephants and albatrosses. He could travel to wild, unexplored places and eat exotic foods called aubergines, capsicums and mushrooms. Suidae was as remarkable a country as any place he'd read about. And he'd read hundreds of interesting books. If only his own life had one brief moment of excitement to match them.

One day, I'll understand all this, Francis thought miserably. One day I'll even work out why I'm alive.

7

PIG TALK

Reg knocked gently on the bedroom door. 'Lucy, are you OK?'

'Yeah,' came the muffled reply. 'Come in.'

As he entered the room, Lucy turned from staring out the window and managed a brief smile.

'Vittoria told me you're feeling crook,' Reg said. 'You all right?' Reg pulled a chair closer to the bed and sat down.

'Yeah, I'm OK. I just didn't want to talk when I came back inside.' Lucy struggled to get her thoughts together. 'Uncle Reg, do you give your pigs names?'

'No. Except for Matilda,' he added. 'But she's

a bit different. She's been around so long I had to call her something.'

'So, you'd give every pig a name if you were keeping them for some reason?'

'Luce, you develop a bond with them. I like giving them a pat and, well, they respond to that,' Reg explained. 'But hundreds of pigs go through here each year. It'd be too much trouble to name them all. Why d'you ask?'

'Well, there's one pig ... one of Dr Price's pigs. He has a name.'

'You mean Francis?'

'You know him?'

'Sure. Been there about twelve months. Nice-looking animal. His father was one of my best boars.'

'And his mother?' Lucy asked with keen interest.

'Guess! Our Matilda.'

'Wow!' Lucy exclaimed. 'So, Francis is one of her piglets?'

Reg considered his reply before answering. 'Yeah, in a way, but it's a little different with those pigs in the laboratory.'

'Laboratory?' Lucy was surprised at this description of the building. It made it sound like a place for experiments, not somewhere for breeding pigs.

'That's what Dr Price calls it. It's not a piggery, like mine is. The pigs in her place are grown from eggs taken from my sows, fertilised in test tubes or something and transplanted back into the mothers.' Reg seemed a bit embarrassed. 'You know all about that stuff?'

'Where we come from?' Lucy replied. 'Sure, we did that at school – and Mum's always talking about it. Now I'm getting older.'

Reg nodded. This sounded like a chat she should be having with her aunt. 'Is that what you want to talk about? Growing up and babies and –'

'I want to talk about Francis,' Lucy interrupted. 'You don't think there's something strange about him?' A talking pig was too ridiculous for words, especially one that talked weird like Francis. But it was hard to ask Uncle Reg directly without sounding like a dingbat.

'He seems OK to me,' Reg replied. 'Never seen him close up though.'

'He hasn't made any strange sounds before?'

'Nup. Why, is he sick or something?'

'No. I don't think so,' Lucy added hastily. 'But what about his pen? He's got a light and a bookstand in it. That's pretty strange, isn't it?'

'Dr Price spends a fair bit of time with

Francis. She keeps that stuff in there so she can make notes and stuff. Anyway, that's what she told me.' Reg shrugged. 'Who can tell what these scientific types get up to?'

Lucy nodded in agreement. That was it really: what was Dr Price up to?

'Look, if Dr Price's pigs are bothering you, I can probably handle them,' Reg offered. 'You go over and play with Sara and Andy, enjoy yourself.'

'I'm too old to play.'

'Well, visit them. I can manage.'

Lucy considered her options and decided her friends would just have to wait. How often did you get a chance to meet a pig like Francis? 'I don't mind the pigs, Uncle Reg. I'd like to keep feeding them.'

'Suit yourself.' Reg stood up. 'You want to come and check those piglets with me?'

'That'd be great.'

Lucy grabbed her shoes. A bit of activity might stop these questions buzzing around her brain. Like, how could a pig talk without being some sort of freak? *How could a pig even talk*? Since her last visit, this had become one crazy farm.

8

A FRIEND IN DEED

Lucy felt more determined in the cool morning light. The sun crept over the hill behind the laboratory as she walked quickly towards the main gate. After her confusing meeting with Francis yesterday, she had avoided looking at him at the noon and evening feeding sessions. And she'd used the time to think.

From what she could work out, Dr Price must be doing some kind of experiments with the pigs. Otherwise, why would Uncle Reg call the building a 'laboratory'? Though, what Dr Price was up to was anyone's guess.

Lucy punched in the code for the roll-a-door, and when it was open enough, ducked inside.

She checked the gauge on the food hopper – it showed half full. There was plenty in there to keep the pigs fed for the rest of the day.

She opened the fuse box, grabbed the ring of keys from inside and let herself into the feeding room. As she changed, the lights flickered on above the pig pens. Lucy remembered that they came on automatically at exactly six o'clock. Dr Price said the computer system created a regular day-and-night world so that the pigs could live as naturally as possible.

Dressed properly, Lucy started the mixing machinery, pressed the red AUTOMATIC FEEDING button and moved towards the glass door. She'd made one important decision – she would talk to Francis. The time for avoiding him was over.

'Dr Price, would you like a cup of tea?'

She woke from her cramped position in the armchair, yawned, and looked up at the nurse.

'Thanks, yes, I would.' She took the cup and the nurse smiled and quietly left the room. Amanda heard the nurse's shoes patter off down the hospital corridor.

She took a few sips of the hot tea. When she came to the city for the weekend, she spent most of her time at the hospital. If it got too late, she often slept beside Henry's bed, just to be with him. Refreshed a little, she rose, walked a few paces and stretched her back.

'Mum? Are you there, Mum?'

Amanda turned towards the bed and Henry lifted his bald head from the pillow. She still hadn't got used to seeing him without his mop of fair, curly hair.

'You all right, darling?'

'Yeah, but I need to go. Real quick.'

'Well, get your slippers on and I'll go with you.'

Henry slowly swung his thin legs over the side of the bed, found the slippers and held out his hand to his mother. She led him out into the corridor.

'I can go into the bathroom myself, Mum. I'll be all right.'

She let him walk on ahead. He's too skinny and too sick for a boy of eleven, she thought. A brain tumour wasn't fair at any age, but it was doubly unfair for someone so young.

She stopped. Thinking about it upset her

once more. There's only one thing I can do, she thought, and I can't put it off much longer. Henry has to have another operation soon – or die.

Francis poked out his tongue and turned the page of the book.

He'd seen the girl enter the feeding room and, out of the corner of his eye, had watched her walk through the glass door and down the aisle towards him. It occurred to him that she probably hadn't expected him to talk and so had been frightened off yesterday. But after all, she'd started it. However, there's no excuse for rudeness, Francis decided. This time I'm going to ignore her.

'Hullo, piggy ... are ... are you really reading that book?' Lucy asked nervously. She rested her hands on the top rail and looked into his pen.

Oh no, we're still calling me *piggy*, Francis sneered to himself. This left him no choice. 'No, I'm going to eat it for dessert.'

There's no imagining this, Lucy thought, this pig is talking. And he's a grouch.

'Just so you know, my handle's Francis,' he snapped. 'Francis Bacon. What's yours?'

'Why do you talk like that?' Lucy asked. 'Cool, dag, handle and all that?'

'That's hip talk, isn't it? Being groovy. Isn't that how you speak in the fast lane?'

'You only say things like that ... sometimes.'

'I wanted to start things off on the right ... foot,' Francis replied crisply. 'Is foot OK?'

'Foot's fine.'

'It's remarkable how many expressions mention parts of the body,' Francis expounded. 'You know – keep at arm's length, put your finger on something, put your shoulders to the wheel, put your best foot forward. Get what I mean?'

'Yeah, I get it.' It was her turn to be impatient. 'This is crazy – you're talking!'

'So are you.'

'But you're a pig! Do the other pigs in here talk?'

'No,' Francis sighed. 'Actually, they don't want to communicate at all. They mainly grunt about food, mealtimes – and food. Pretty pathetic really.'

'You talk ... pig talk ... too?'

'I'm bilingual. It's a pity we don't talk more, because pig language is more complex than you'd think,' Francis explained. 'There's just not much to talk about in here. However, personally, I'm trying to brush up my Italian and French too.'

Lucy stared at him in disbelief. I'm talking to a pig, a live, speaking animal. A pig who seems smarter than anyone I've ever met. And worse, she was even thinking of him as *who*, when her teacher always said animals were *which*. 'But I still don't get it – how come you can talk?'

Francis didn't feel so irritated now that this girl seemed genuinely interested in him. This was shaping up to be a pretty reasonable conversation.

'Well, I've wondered about that too – once I *could* talk. I guess I was born to talk. And Dr Price taught me to read too. She started about nine months ago.'

'Francis, it's not usual for pigs to talk – in any language.' Now I'm calling him Francis, she thought. How can I tell Uncle Reg I've spent the morning talking to a pig?

'I have no way of judging that,' Francis replied. 'I've only ever lived here. I can't comment on other pigs.'

'I've seen about a thousand pigs,' Lucy stated. 'And none of them talk to people. Z-E-R-O. None.'

Francis suspected she was right. He'd read fairy tales and myths about talking animals, but in no other book had he ever found an example of real animals talking, except for budgies and parrots. It seemed fair enough to ask her about that. 'What about budgies and parrots?' he said.

'They're like ... what do you call them? Mimics,' Lucy replied. 'They don't really make up sentences or think like you do. They just learn a few phrases and repeat them.'

Francis had to admit that seemed a likely explanation. 'That would make me pretty unique, wouldn't it?'

'Unreal, more like it.'

Francis was silent for a while. If she was right, and he was the only talking pig in the world, then it all seemed a bit pointless. He was trapped in a pen with nothing to do and nowhere to go. Maybe it was some kind of punishment? Like Oliver Twist in the poorhouse.

'Francis, are you OK?' Lucy asked.

'Yes, I expect so.' He tried to forget his unpleasant thoughts. He looked at the girl. She was no thicko, no old foge. She seemed to be on his wavelength. Maybe this was a real chance to make a friend. 'So, what's your name?'

'I'm Lucy. Lucinda Russo.'

'Russo is Italian for Russian,' Francis informed her. 'So, you're Lucinda the Russian. Do Lucinda's come in other nationalities too?'

'Don't ask me.'

'And Lucinda means light. Are you a Light Russian?'

Lucy laughed. 'My mum and dad are Italian. They never said anything about being Russian. And they've lived in Australia since they were little kids. Why are *you* called Francis Bacon?'

'I figure Dr Price named me after the famous seventeenth century English philosopher,' Francis suggested. 'Or possibly the twentieth century British artist. What do you think?'

'Beats me. I've never heard of either one.'

'The original Francis Bacon was quite famous,' Francis went on. 'Some people say he wrote some of William Shakespeare's plays.'

'Wow! Did he?'

'No,' Francis said. 'He wasn't a good enough writer, in my opinion. Do you read much?'

'A bit. I watch a lot of TV.'

'Is it any good?'

'Yeah, but Mum says I'm always watching too much of it.'

'And are you?'

'Sure,' Lucy replied. 'But I do other stuff. I play soccer and basketball too.'

'While you're watching TV?'

'You can't do them all at once!'

'Don't snap at me,' Francis protested. 'I've never been out of here. How would I know?'

Lucy could see he had a point. 'Sorry, but everyone's always having a go at me about TV.'

'I've read a lot about TV,' Francis said. 'Leading critics believe it makes you stupid and moronic. Does it?'

'Sure.' Lucy assumed a really dumb expression and stuck her tongue out the side of her mouth.

Francis didn't know how to react. 'Is that meant to be funny?'

'Most people would laugh.'

Francis made an effort to curl up his lips and bare his teeth. 'How's that?'

'OK, but you'll have to work on your sense of humour. Anyway, I better go.'

'Will you come and ... hang out ... again?'

'I'm not really supposed to. Doesn't Dr

Price talk to you?'

'I think she has a lot on her mind,' Francis replied unhappily. 'She hardly ever stops by any more.'

His brown eyes filled with tears and Lucy reached out and stroked his head. 'I'll come back this afternoon. I promise.'

'I'm sorry if I was cranky earlier on.'

'That's OK.'

'When you come back – can you do me a favour?'

'Sure.'

'There should be some new books in Dr Price's office. Can you get them for me?' Francis asked. 'They help pass the time.' He glanced towards a door only a few metres away, on the opposite side from the feeding room. 'Her office is over there.'

'OK.'

'See you ... dag,' Francis said with a crinkly smile.

'Bye ... piggy,' Lucy said softly.

9
A DOCTORED DREAM

Francis was taking an afternoon nap as Lucy crept by.

Uncle Reg had told her once that pigs spent more time resting than any other domesticated animal. If they weren't eating, they were sleeping. With all the zzz's floating around the laboratory, it was obvious these pigs were no exception.

On reaching the office, Lucy fumbled with the keys nervously. Even though Dr Price was away, she was taking a risk. The third key she tried opened the door.

There was a desk and chair by the window, but the room, almost completely white, was more than an office. Along the other three walls were benches covered with heaps of scientific equipment. There were two big microscopes, an electronic weighing machine, lots of glass tubes, flasks and measuring cylinders. And, under one bench, Lucy spotted a small fridge.

A box of books sat on the desk. Lucy quickly grabbed a couple for Francis, but something made her stop and look more carefully.

The box was marked HENRY & FRANCIS with red pen. That's strange, thought Lucy. What was the connection between the books, Francis and Dr Price's son? More curious than ever, she scanned the office and saw a chart pinned to the wall.

It was a plan of the pig pen area, showing which ones were occupied. The pen numbered B2 had a red sticker on it and a yellow post-it note saying TRANSPORT ARRANGED MONDAY – FURTHER RESEARCH. So, that was what the red stickers meant, Lucy realised. But what sort of research was planned for the pig?

Her eyes moved along the chart. In a column marked DECEASED there was a line of ten red stickers. Deceased meant *dead*, didn't it? Lucy shuddered and gripped the books tightly. She crossed to the door and slammed it behind her.

Ignoring Francis, she dumped the books in his pen and ran from the laboratory.

Lucy heard the loud squeaking of brakes as she ate her breakfast. When Amanda's voice carried into the house, her heart raced.

'Can I finish this in a minute?' She dropped the spoon into her cereal and left the room.

'Lucy – where are you going?' Vittoria called and then looked over at Reg. 'What's all that about?'

'Don't ask me.' He casually turned the page of his newspaper. 'Any more toast?'

Outside, Lucy jogged towards the laboratory. A white van was parked in the loading bay. Everything to do with this Genius Genes crowd seems to be white, she thought. Maybe they wanted the world to think that everything they did was good and pure. She had a feeling the Corporation was up to something pretty fishy.

Lucy halted at the gate. There was no-one

about and she guessed that Dr Price had gone inside. She had no choice; she'd have to wait.

The racket woke Francis from a fitful sleep. All night he'd been dreaming of spaghetti and movies and swimming at the beach. He often had this dream.

It always started somewhere in Italy, like the Colosseum or the Leaning Tower of Pisa. Then he'd be flying. He'd jump into the air, flap his ears and float over all the lands and oceans till he got to Australia.

After that, the dream got jumbled. Sometimes, he'd be floating on a tyre in the sea, eating spaghetti from a trough and watching a movie screen set up in the sandhills, hundreds of metres away. And other pigs would row past him, speaking Italian and eating popcorn.

Other times, he would be rowing a boat through a sea of spaghetti. And a whole lot of movie screens would be bobbing on the surface, like buoys. But no matter how hard he rowed, Francis never got close enough to see what films were showing on the screens. At this stage he usually woke up, frustrated.

However, this morning he was woken by the sound of someone opening the gates of B2, one of the pig pens in his row. Francis stood on the bottom rail and craned his neck for a better look.

'Just this one,' Amanda was telling two men. 'And she goes to our city headquarters. Rear entrance. OK?'

'OK, Doc, whatever you say,' one of the men replied.

The six-month-old sow squealed as she was lifted into a padded wooden crate with wheels fixed to its base. One of the men nailed on the lid, and the sow gave a loud screech. It set off a chorus of shrill replies from the other pigs.

Francis kept quiet. It's happening again, he thought, this is the fifth pig to be taken away in two months. But where was she going? GENIUS GENES CORPORATION was stencilled in black on the crate, but there were no other clues to its destination.

'Get her out quickly, please,' Amanda demanded. 'It upsets the other pigs.'

The men quickly pushed the crate towards the glass doors, and in a few seconds, they were out of sight.

Amanda turned to Francis and gave him a long, serious look – a peculiar, questioning expression that he'd never seen before. She turned and walked outside.

Francis frowned. Why had Dr Price looked at him so strangely? Usually, he felt very hungry after one of his spaghetti dreams. Now, as he looked at the fresh food in the trough, he realised his appetite was gone.

Lucy saw the large crate, pushed by two workmen, appear in the loading bay.

They lifted it into the back of the van and locked the door. With a farewell nod to Amanda, they climbed into the van and backed it onto the roadway. As it drove off, Amanda looked angrily at Lucy.

'Lucy, come here, please!' she called out. 'I want a word with you.'

10

WHO'S HENRY?

'You've been speaking to Francis, haven't you?'
Amanda said.

Lucy avoided her eyes.

'I noticed a couple of books had gone from my
office. And you left these in the door.' Amanda
held up the bunch of keys. 'It didn't take much
to make the connection with you, Lucy.'

'I'm sorry, I didn't mean to –'

'I told you not to go into the pig pen area. Do
you know why?'

'I suppose you didn't want me to find Francis,'
Lucy replied guiltily.

'Well, you're partly right. I didn't want you to
meet Francis, but there's another reason. I

don't want those pigs disturbed. Or to risk any contamination from outside germs. They've been bred for a specific purpose.'

'Yeah, I know. You want to kill them.'

Amanda looked surprised. She hadn't counted on Lucy being curious at all. She'd expected Lucy would just feed the pigs and get on with her holiday. 'I think I should explain a few things to you,' she said. 'Then you might understand.'

'Explain what?' Lucy asked. 'All I want to know is – what are you going to do to Francis?'

'Can I make a deal with you?' Amanda bargained.

Lucy wasn't sure how to answer that. She liked Francis and she didn't want him hurt or harmed in any way, but it would be difficult to keep seeing him, without going along with Dr Price. 'What sort of deal?'

'I'll tell you everything about Francis, about what I'm doing,' Amanda said, 'if you'll do three things.'

'What?'

'Swear you'll keep my work a secret and not talk to anyone about Francis and his ... his true abilities.'

Lucy figured this wasn't a hard promise to keep, no-one would believe her anyway. And she was keen to find out about Dr Price's research. 'OK. What's the third?'

'There is *one* thing I'd like you to do.'

'What?'

'I'm going to the city tomorrow and I'd like you to come with me,' Amanda said. 'There's someone I want you to meet.'

'I don't get it. Why did you bring me here?' Lucy asked Amanda as they left the elevator on the second floor of the Children's Hospital.

Lucy hated hospitals. Ever since breaking her arm in Year 3, the smell, the sound and the look of them made her want to vomit. If I'd known this was going to be part of my vow of silence, she thought, I'd have held out for a better deal.

And she hated her dress. It scratched her neck and had frills and bows that were really lumpy to sit on. Especially when travelling two hundred k's by car. Dr Price must have told Aunt Vittoria they were going to the ballet or something.

Amanda led the way down the corridor. 'Just

up here on the left, Lucy.' She stepped into the next room and, reluctantly, Lucy followed. A thin, bald-headed boy of about her own age was lying in bed, reading a book.

'Lucy, I'd like you to meet my son. Henry, this is Lucy Russo.'

'Hi,' Lucy said politely.

The boy in the bed said nothing.

'Henry? I've brought someone to see you.' Amanda squeezed his hand to attract his attention. Finally, he put down the book and looked at Lucy. 'Hullo, nice of you to come,' he said unemotionally.

'That's OK.' Uh-oh, this is a set-up to make me feel bad, Lucy guessed. Dr Price wants me to see what a hard time she's having with her son. All this is to stop me blabbing about Francis.

'I'll have to leave you two for a minute.' Amanda turned to Lucy and said, 'I have to see Henry's father. He's a surgeon here.'

She kissed Henry on the cheek and left. Lucy was close to the bed and could see some scars on Henry's head. 'If you don't mind me asking, what are the scars from?'

'Brain tumour,' Henry replied. 'I've had a

couple of operations.'

'Did they shave your head?'

'Fell out. The chemotherapy makes your hair fall out.'

'Oh. So, how are you getting on?' Lucy knew the question was lame, but it was hard to think of something to say.

'Pretty bad, I s'pose,' Henry said. 'I haven't been out of here in two months and I'd really like to go to the beach.'

'Can't you go out sometimes?'

'No, my resistance is way down. If I leave here, I'll probably get pneumonia and die.' He smiled in a peculiar way. 'I'm probably gonna die anyway.'

'How long have you had it? The ...' Lucy couldn't bring herself to say 'the tumour'.

'Couple of years. They thought they'd got it the first time. But the operations never seem to do any good.'

Lucy noticed a pile of books on the cupboard by Henry's bed – Oliver Twist, some Hardy Boy mysteries and some others that looked familiar. She'd seen the same books either being read by Francis or in the box on Dr Price's desk.

'What's this like?' she asked, picking up *Oliver Twist*. 'Any good?'

'Yeah, it's a classic. Do you read much?'

'A bit. I watch a lot of TV.'

'I've read a lot about TV,' Henry said. 'Leading critics believe it makes you stupid and moronic. Does it?'

This is really weird, Lucy thought. Not only the same books, but I'm having the same conversation I had with Francis. 'No, it's great,' she answered sarcastically. 'You get home from school, you switch it on and you can watch it for hours. Flick all the channels. I love it, it's great.'

Henry went quiet again and stared out the window. 'I haven't had any fun for a long time. Movies, swimming ... nothing.'

Lucy wished she hadn't sounded off like that and Henry picked up on her mood. 'Don't feel sorry for me. Getting a tumour's just one of those things. Mum and Dad worry about it more than I do. All I want ... is to get out of here.'

Lucy touched Henry's hand. 'I hope you get better soon, I really do.'

'Thanks.'

'How are you two getting on?' Amanda's

voice came from the doorway.

'OK.' Henry looked directly at Lucy. 'You can come and visit me again. If you want to.'

'Lucy?' Amanda asked pointedly.

Lucy smiled awkwardly at her while she thought about Henry and Francis. She'd been worrying about the hospital and her dress. Faced with their problems, she had no worries at all.

11
PIGS AND PEOPLE

A single bright light shone in the laboratory as Francis stood in his pen and stared thoughtfully into the darkness. The main lights had gone off an hour ago and Francis had switched on his lamp. The other pigs had quickly fallen asleep. There were only two things occupying his mind – the arrival of Lucy Russo into his life and his chances of getting outside.

About six weeks ago, he'd first thought about escaping into the world after reading the story of the Count of Monte Christo.

It was about this young Frenchman who is sent to prison for a crime he didn't do. He befriends a wise older man and they start digging a tunnel. Before they can escape, the old man dies and the guards sew his body into a sack. The Frenchman takes out the body, hides it in the tunnel, and gets inside the sack himself. After the guards toss it into the sea, he crawls out and swims away. Later, the Frenchman finds a secret treasure and becomes famous as the Count of Monte Christo. Francis smiled as he remembered the details. It was a great story.

However, reading the book had been a good and a bad experience. Bad, because Francis started to think of his pen as a prison cell. For weeks, the idea of a tunnel appealed to him as a way out. Not to escape; just a tunnel that he could use to go outside on visits. To take in the sights, or to go for walks under the stars at night.

For a week, he tested every corner of the pen – the floor, the railings and the gate; even under the feeding trough. He'd tried chewing away at a few spots, but everything was made of steel. After chipping a tooth, he'd given up.

Next, he tried climbing out of the pen in the middle of the night. But he'd grown fairly big and his legs weren't strong enough to lift his weight over the top rail. He gave up on that too.

And two weeks ago, the cleaner had left the pen's gate open when she came to scour his trough. He'd raced for the opening, but slipped on a long piece of apple peel and fell flat on his face. The cleaner banged the gate shut and he'd missed his chance.

Tonight, under the light of the lamp, Francis felt new hope. And that's where Lucy came into the picture. Meeting her was like the Count of Monte Christo meeting the wise old man in prison. Lucy would help him get out of here.

Lucy finished her second helping of apple pie and cream. In a second, the dark-suited waiter was at her side and whisked away the empty bowl.

'Would you like more drinks, Madam?' His question was directed at Amanda.

'Not for me, thank you. Lucy?'

'I'm OK, thanks.' Lucy didn't want to say it, but after soup, main course and two desserts, she was bloated. And this was the sort of place where you had to watch your manners.

Important-looking people talked quietly at the other tables and there were mirrors, chandeliers and shining cutlery all over the place. It was the swankiest restaurant she'd ever seen.

Amanda wiped her mouth with a napkin and folded it onto the table. 'So, tell me, Lucy. What do you know about science?'

'Not much. We've done stuff on biology and the environment at school,' she replied.

'Well, that's a start. Do you want to hear about my work?'

This is what I've been waiting for all day, Lucy thought. But she had to concentrate hard. After the long drive and the visit to the hospital, she was tired. 'Can I ask something first? What sort of doctor did you say you were?'

'I'm a biochemist, basically, though I've had a little bit of medical training. My work involves chemistry, you know, the way chemicals and substances work together. Except I'm interested in how it affects living things.'

'Like – the pigs?'

'Yes, especially the pigs.' Amanda leaned forward and looked Lucy in the eyes. 'I'll explain exactly what I'm doing. Maybe one day you'll get interested in this line of work yourself.'

That's about as likely as me volunteering for the space program, Lucy thought. Still, I better go along with her. 'I like Maths – and I sort of like History and English sometimes.'

'In that case, I'll speak in straightforward English,' Amanda said. 'The pigs in the laboratory are specially bred pigs –'

'I gathered that after talking to Francis –'

'Francis is even more special than the others,' Amanda interrupted. 'But they all have one thing in common. They're what scientists call *transgenic* pigs.'

'What's trans ... that?'

'Have you heard about genes?'

'Yeah, they're blue with holes in the knees.'

'I like that.' Amanda smiled. 'I must use it in my next speech. But I'm talking about g-e-n-e-s. And a thing called genetic engineering.'

'Is that what you're doing with the pigs?'

'Yes. Do you know much about cells?'

'Our body is made up of billions of them,' Lucy replied. 'Our heart and muscles and stuff are all different cells.'

'Right.' Amanda unfolded her napkin and

spread it out on the table. She took a pen from her pocket and drew a big circle on it. 'Let's say this is a cell. Inside every cell in the body there are forty-six separate bits called chromosomes.'

'I've heard about them,' Lucy stated.

'Good. And each chromosome has a long piece of DNA inside it, and they're shaped in what's called a double helix pattern.'

Amanda scribbled the shape alongside the circle that represented the cell.

'And even smaller parts of the DNA are called genes. There are thousands of tiny little genes. OK?'

Lucy nodded.

'The genes are the things that help to form

all the parts of our body. There are genes for our heart, our stomach, our kidneys, the liver, the brain, the bones. Everything.'

'I get that.'

'But what I'm doing in the laboratory is making some new genes to put inside the pigs. I'm taking tiny bits of the human genes that make up our liver, heart, kidneys and other organs, and I'm putting them into the pigs.'

Lucy squirmed in her chair. 'You mean ... all your pigs are sort of human?'

'In a way. They're almost 100 percent pig, but in some organs of their body, part of their cells are human. Very tiny, important bits. That's what I mean by transgenic. It means part of the pig comes from another species. In this case, human beings.'

'But why?' Lucy wasn't sure if she was fascinated or sickened by the idea. 'It's such a weird thing to do.'

'You know about transplants?' Amanda asked. 'People getting kidneys and hearts and things from other people?'

'After road accidents and that?'

'Yes. Look, there are more people wanting organs than there are organs available. There are hundreds of people who are waiting for kidney transplants alone. But there aren't enough people donating them and it's a big problem. Sometimes patients have to stay on dialysis machines for years.'

'But what have your pigs got to do with that?' Lucy asked.

'Think about it,' Amanda continued. 'If we can breed hundreds of transgenic pigs, with kidneys, hearts or livers that are partly human, then we can transplant them into people. That's what my research is about. We can't wait till people die in car accidents; we have to find a way of getting more donor organs. That's what I'm trying to do with the pigs.'

'Is that what the Genius Genes Corporation is all about?' Lucy queried.

'Yes. They're a group of businessmen who pay for my research.'

'And they're going to make heaps of money out of giving people new kidneys and livers and stuff?'

'That's exactly what they're going to do,' Amanda confessed. 'Medicine is big money these days. We spend billions on hospitals and various drugs and operations to cure people. I'm just part of it.'

This is mind-boggling, Lucy thought. I've heard about mad scientists who do evil things, but what about scientists who do things for money? Was that right? And Dr Price, dressed in her neat jacket and skirt, looked as normal as you could get.

'I can tell you more if you like. Back at the laboratory, I can show you how transgenics works. Are you interested?' Amanda asked.

'Yeah, I am.' Lucy felt uneasy. 'Tell me one thing, Dr Price. Why have so many pigs died? All those red stickers ...'

'My research is risky,' Amanda explained. 'Unfortunately, some of the experiments are fatal.'

'What about Francis?' Lucy demanded. 'What are you going to do with him?'

Amanda was silent for a moment. 'Francis is different. He's part of a different project altogether.'

12
HOME AND AWAY

Lucy hadn't expected the laboratory to feel so creepy at night. The eerie infra-red light that came from a few bulbs on the ceiling sent shivers down her spine.

She'd just got back from her trip to the city with Dr Price. After saying goodnight to Uncle Reg and Aunt Vittoria, she'd waited a few minutes and then climbed out of her bedroom window.

Lucy changed into her overalls and boots, and a minute later, she found Francis gently snoring in his pen. His chest rose and fell slowly and his breath whistled comically through his nostrils.

When she'd first heard Francis talk, he seemed totally off-the-planet, even frightening. Now, he was just a pig who could read and talk. In a way, I could be looking at Aunt Vittoria or Uncle Reg, Lucy thought. Especially since he's partly human.

A tightness gripped her chest as she remembered her talk with Dr Price. She'd been tired and had not really taken in what Dr Price said about Francis – *He's part of a different project altogether.* Lucy kicked herself for not finding out more. She felt sure that whatever the project was, Francis was in danger.

'It's gross,' she said, sighing deeply.

The sound of her voice woke Francis. He blinked several times. 'Is that you, Lucy?'

'Sorry to wake you. I just wanted to see you. I –'

'I wanted to see you too ...' Francis said at the same time. 'Sorry, you go first.'

'What were you going to say?'

'I've been thinking,' Francis said, 'about where the pigs go. Did you see that sow leave yesterday?'

'I saw a crate being carried out. Was that her?'

'Yes. I've often wondered about where they

go. Maybe they go to a farm somewhere?' Francis suggested.

Lucy didn't want to answer the question.

'And then I thought about us ...'

'What about us?'

'We could go and visit them,' he explained. 'I'd really like to see where they end up. And, I thought you could come here some nights and let me out and we could go for walks and we could explore –'

'I don't know if that's such a good idea,' Lucy cut in.

'Why?'

'I don't think Dr Price would like it.' How could she explain what she already knew about Dr Price's work?

The pigs weren't going to a farm; they were heading straight to another laboratory in the city. And dying there.

'I suppose you're right,' Francis muttered. 'I was just hoping we could go out, like friends do.' He looked at her inquiringly. 'Do you have many friends?'

'Sure.' In fact, she was popular. 'But I'm just as happy by myself, or with friends. Why do you want to know?'

'Well, I think our lives were meant to come together,' Francis said emphatically.

'Why do you think that?'

'Meetings between like-minded people, or pigs, don't happen by chance.' He warmed to the subject. 'It's fate. I figure you've been sent to take me into the world. Have you heard of the Count of Monte Christo?'

'Who's he?'

She listened as Francis briefly explained the story. 'You see, Lucy, there's a lot out there and I want to see it. You can help me.'

'Francis, life's not like a book,' Lucy said seriously. 'The real world's not all fun and adventures, especially for pigs.'

'What do you mean?'

'I can't explain it properly. But it can be dangerous, you might get hurt.' He has no idea what's in store for him, Lucy reflected unhappily. Not that I know exactly either. But judging by the luck of the other pigs, it won't be good.

'How will I get hurt?'

'Look, can we talk about this later?' Lucy said. 'I better get to bed.'

'OK. But ... are we friends now?'

'Yeah, we're friends.' Lucy rubbed his snout affectionately. 'Night.'

Matilda shook herself like a wet dog, sending showers of water all around the shed.

Lucy jumped back from the spray. 'Thanks a lot, Matilda.'

'Come on, Matilda, take it easy old girl,' Reg said soothingly. 'More water on her back.'

Lucy directed the hose at Matilda's fat, wobbly bottom. The sow oinked and wriggled with pleasure as Reg scrubbed her skin with a wooden brush. The water cascaded over the sow's back and gurgled down the drain. Hosing down the pigs was part of readying them for the Show, though Lucy was never quite sure who ended up cleaner and wetter – the pigs or her.

'We'll give the piglets a bit of a scrub before we put them onto the truck tomorrow,' Reg said. 'We'll have to leave early, Luce.'

'That's OK, I don't mind.'

The only thing she was worried about was not seeing Francis while they were in the city. They'd have to stay with the pigs at the showgrounds for at least three or four days.

Who'd keep an eye on Francis while she was away? What if he was carted off by those workmen?

'OK, that'll do it.' Reg put down the brush. 'You can turn the hose off.'

'You want to do the boars today?' Lucy asked.

'Yeah, this afternoon.' He planned to enter five of his other champion pigs as well.

'Can I go now?'

'Could use a help with the feed,' Reg said gruffly.

'I have to see Dr Price,' Lucy replied. 'She wants to have a talk.' Lucy was dying to say something, but remembered her vow of silence.

'You two are getting quite chummy,' Reg stated. 'Lucky to get any help from you these days.' A quick smile showed that he wasn't really having a go at her.

'We're not friends or anything,' Lucy explained. 'It's just that I'm interested in what she's doing. It's sort of ... educational.' Using that word would get her off the hook. 'Educational' excused almost anything as far as adults were concerned.

'Well, don't let me stand in the way of progress,' Reg replied encouragingly. 'Go on – get going.'

A big black limousine was parked just inside the gates of the laboratory. Lucy could see the chauffeur asleep behind the wheel, a cap shading his eyes. He must have brought visitors, she decided, important ones by the look of the car.

Once inside, there was no mistaking the unhappy look on Francis's face. 'Hi,' she whispered. 'You OK?'

'It's gross, dumb and a bungle,' he complained. 'Dr Price has nicked my books and taken my lamp away.'

'This got anything to do with the visitors?'

'Think so,' he muttered. 'She came in this morning and just took my stuff away. And the name card from my pen. She didn't say a thing.'

Lucy checked – the card *had* gone. 'So, who's in there?'

'Three men in suits. I think they're from the Genius Genes Corporation,' Francis said.

Lucy glanced at the office door. There was

only one possible conclusion – Dr Price was keeping Francis a secret from the visitors. But why? 'Just wait here.'

'Where do you think I'm going – Hawaii?'

Lucy ignored the crack and walked over to the office. She knocked loudly on the door.

'Come in,' she heard Amanda call faintly.

Lucy pushed the door inwards and four heads turned to look at her.

'Hullo, Lucy,' Amanda said stiffly. 'Look, I'm busy at the moment.' The sight of the young interloper held no interest for the three men and they turned back to study the pig charts on the noticeboard. Two of the men were dark-haired, and the third one had reddish hair and a beard. They were all dressed exactly the same, in dark-blue suits and striped ties. 'Could you do me a favour and come back later this afternoon?' Amanda requested. 'I'm going to be rather busy till then.'

'Sure, no worries,' Lucy replied cheerfully.

Amanda turned back to the noticeboard.

Lucy pretended to close the door, but left it slightly open and listened.

'How close are we now to the first transplant operations?' A man with a deep voice asked.

'About two months,' Amanda replied. 'We have to find volunteers, but I don't think that will be a problem. We can work through a private hospital.'

'What about that big male pig out there?' another voice asked. 'The one in B5.'

Lucy guessed they were talking about Francis.

'My husband, Ross, and I have been carrying out some vital research in that area,' Amanda said. 'But I think it's too early to draw any conclusions.'

'He's expensive to keep,' the deep voice said.

'I know. We've spent a lot on him,' Amanda continued, 'but he's reached the right size and weight now.'

'So why are we keeping him here?' a third voice asked. 'We can't feed him for ever.'

'He has some extra genetic material that needs further testing. But it won't be long, I assure you. I think he'll repay all the effort we've put into him.'

Lucy thought she could detect a note of worry in Amanda's voice.

'I think we should leave him in Amanda's capable hands,' the deep voice said pleasantly.

'I'm sure when the time's right, she'll do what she has to.'

'Yes, thank you, Brian, I will,' came her relieved reply.

'Meanwhile,' the third voice said, 'we'll make plans to market your research. There's big money to be made from this organ transplant business. And we'll be in on it first.'

'People will queue up to pay a fortune,' Brian boasted. 'We'll be millionaires in no time.'

'Billionaires more like it!' All the men laughed heartily.

Lucy closed the door quietly and walked back to Francis's pen.

'So, what's up?' he asked.

'I'll see you later; I have to help Uncle Reg.'

She smiled awkwardly at Francis and went quickly away.

Thanks a lot, I'm back where I started, Francis thought, now everyone's ignoring me. No name, no books, no conversation. Zilch.

He sighed. Maybe Lucy wasn't the one to help him after all.

13
UNDER THE MICROSCOPE

'Lucy, I'm sorry I couldn't talk to you earlier on,' Amanda apologised.

She got up from the desk and walked to a bench on the other side of the office. 'I have these meetings every month and I can't get out of them.'

'That's OK.' As it was late afternoon, Lucy was disappointed to find that Dr Price hadn't gone home to her flat in Makinville. She'd hoped to have another snoop around.

'Come and see this.' Amanda sat in front of one of the microscopes and picked up a small glass slide. Lucy closed the door and joined her. 'I think the best way to explain things is to show you what I do,' Amanda said. 'Take a peek.'

There were two sets of viewing lenses, like pairs of binoculars, built into the microscope. Amanda looked through the top ones and Lucy used the set at the side. 'What do you see?'

The bright light magnified a single cell with a cluster of tiny particles in its centre.

'Some sort of cell, isn't it?' Lucy asked.

'It's a new, single egg that I've taken from a sow. It's just been fertilised by sperm from a boar, and now I'm going to carry out the next step.'

Amanda picked up a special eye-dropper with a narrow piece of glass tubing at the end, thinner than a cotton thread. 'This is called a pipette. Watch what I do.'

Lucy squinted into the lens and saw the end of the pipette poke through the outside wall of the cell.

Amanda squeezed the rubber bulb and a little blob of minute particles flooded into the interior of the cell.

'What's that?' Lucy asked.

'This is how I create a transgenic pig. What I'm doing is putting new genetic material into the cell. This pig will grow up with a partly human liver.'

'I don't get it – how?'

'It's simpler than you think.' Dr Price looked up. 'First, I take chromosomes from human cells – usually mine. Next, I break them up into really tiny, gene-size pieces. Millions of them would fit onto a pinhead.'

'Far out!'

'Then I make a thing called recombinant DNA – don't worry about what that is – and I grow it in one of these flat glass dishes.' Amanda touched a dish on the bench. 'With a special instrument, I find the human genes I'm interested in, say liver genes, and I take them out of the dish. Then I grow lots of them in a flask.'

She indicated a row of glass flasks and tubing at the other end of the bench.

'Is that what genetic engineering is?'

'That's part of it. Then I do exactly the same thing with the liver genes from a pig. And, using a special chemical, I combine part of the human liver genes with part of the pig liver genes. It becomes a combined pig–human liver gene. And that's what I've squirted here into the cell.'

Lucy was silent for a moment. 'But why do you want to do all this?'

'Well, one of the big problems with donating livers, kidneys and hearts is a thing called rejection.'

Rejection sounds like the way I'm treating Francis at the moment, Lucy thought miserably. 'You mean ... some people can't take the organs from someone else?' she guessed.

'Exactly,' Amanda replied. 'In fact, we always have to give the person who's getting a new liver or kidney or something, a special drug to stop the rejection. And, I guess you can imagine the problems we might have if we're transplanting organs from a pig into a human being?'

'It wouldn't work,' Lucy said.

'Not unless we're careful. If the liver growing in a pig is partly human, then when it's transplanted to a human being, it has a greater chance of successfully working inside that person. Do you see that?'

Lucy nodded. It was really bizarre, but it was easier to understand than she thought.

Amanda took a packet of M & M's from a drawer.

'Like some?' She poured a small pile into Lucy's hand.

'It's like one of these,' Amanda said, holding

an M & M between her fingers. 'It has a coating on the outside and chocolate inside.'

'Yeah, I really like them.'

'Well, it's like what I'm doing. When I create one of these special livers inside a pig ... the liver is sort of pig on the inside with a coating of human genetic material on the outside,' she continued. 'So, when the liver is transplanted into a human, there is less chance of it being rejected. The person's body will think it's a human liver.'

'That's unreal.' Lucy didn't want to let on that she'd overheard part of the earlier conversation. 'Have you got it to work yet?'

'No, but I shouldn't have any trouble finding volunteers. There are lots of people needing new livers and kidneys.'

"But what about Francis?' Lucy asked. 'He can talk and that.'

Amanda looked thoughtful. After a few moments' silence, she said, 'Francis has a number of human organs. My research work has gone a long way in the last year or so. And he's the result.'

'He's got a human brain, hasn't he?'

'Yes. And his larynx – his voice box. And his

lungs and a couple of other organs as well.'

'How did you do all that?'

'Much the same way as I've shown you today,' Amanda said. 'Except it took hundreds of hours of work and a lot more human genetic material. No-one has ever achieved what I've done.'

Lucy was careful about her next question. 'Do those men know what you're doing – with Francis? The ones who were here today.'

'Not exactly. I thought I'd experiment first and see if it was successful. It's worked out better than I could have imagined.'

Lucy was frightened. Her worst suspicions were being confirmed. Francis was going to die like the other pigs.

Amanda sensed her doubts. 'Is there something else?'

'Francis and Henry read the same books and say similar things,' Lucy answered. 'How come?'

'The human genetic material in Francis came from Henry,' Amanda said. 'I took cells from Henry's body and bred them up in here.'

'Why do you want Francis to think and talk?'

'I want him to experience and learn all that Henry has.' Amanda suddenly looked tired and worried. 'The operations have all failed and I'm trying to save Henry's life. A year ago, I decided to grow a brain exactly like his in a pig ... inside Francis. And then transplant it back into Henry. Ross is going to do the operation in a few days' time.'

I was right about the immediate danger, Lucy realised. 'Aren't you like ... playing God? Making animals into something they're not?'

'I'm doing exactly what nature has done for millions of years, through evolution.'

'It's not the same though,' Lucy said. 'Pigs don't ... they don't talk and think like people. Ever.'

'In some ways you're right. When I started this work five years ago I thought I'd just help medical science along a bit. With things like organ transplants.' Then she added, 'but that was before Henry got sick.'

She looked at the noticeboard and all the red stickers. Her voice was deeply emotional. 'Am I wrong to want to save my son? Is it wrong to save children from disease if we can do it with genetic engineering?'

Lucy couldn't argue with that. 'But what about Francis?'

'Francis is merely a means to an end,' Amanda said more firmly. 'I want his brain to save my son. My husband is a very clever surgeon and he might just make it work. You do understand?'

Lucy struggled with her emotions. 'I ... I didn't know you could transplant brains.'

'Up till now, it's been impossible,' Dr Price said. 'It's a long and complex operation, but we've worked out a way of rejoining the nerve cells between the brain and the spinal cord, using lasers and microsurgery,' she said. 'We're definitely going to try. We have nothing to lose.'

I've got to stay cool and not panic, Lucy thought. There were only a couple of days, at most, to save Francis. She had to get away quickly and make plans. 'Thanks for talking to me, Dr Price. I really appreciate it,' she said sweetly.

'That's OK,' Amanda replied. 'But it's between you and me. This is our secret.'

'Sure. Anything you say.'

14

MOTHER AND SON

Lucy climbed into the pen and jabbed Francis in the ribs. 'Come on, wake up!'

'Unggghh!' Francis woke with a startled look on his face.

'Francis, I've been talking to you for two minutes. We've got to go!' Lucy urged.

Francis blinked in the dim red light of the laboratory. 'Is that you, Lucy?'

'No, it's Santa Claus – where's my cake?'

'No need to get sarky.' Francis struggled to his feet. 'I'm not a morning pig. What time is it?'

'Five o'clock. Look, do you want to get out of here, or not?'

'I thought you'd forgotten all about that,' Francis

replied sulkily. 'Are we going for a walk?'

'Better than that. A drive.'

'Before breakfast?'

'Francis, if we don't leave, you'll end up as breakfast.'

'What do you mean? Why do you say that?'

'Don't ask any questions now. Come on!' Lucy unlatched the gate and stepped out into the passageway.

Francis wanted to follow, but now he was racked with doubts.

'Are you coming?' Lucy said impatiently.

'What happens to me if I stay here?' he asked anxiously. 'What happens if I go out there?'

I put my foot in it there, Lucy realised, he doesn't know which way to turn. 'Francis, forget what I said, I was only joking,' she said cheerfully. 'Don't you want to see the world? I'm taking you on a trip. To the Easter Show.'

'Oh, really?' His interest again turned quickly to caution. 'What's the Show?'

'It's a big carnival ... and it's fun!'

Francis took a deep breath and a step towards the gate. 'Does Dr Price know about this?'

The question surprised Lucy, but she didn't

hesitate. 'Yep,' she said. 'Get them trotters moving – now!'

The sun was barely up as Reg loaded Matilda and the litter onto the truck. She had a separate pen in the back corner to prevent the piglets getting crushed.

The other sows and boars were already on board, further towards the front, snorting and snuffling amongst the thick pile of straw on the floor.

'Can I sit in with them, like I did last year?' Lucy said, as she appeared from around the side of the truck.

Reg was about to shut the truck's rear gate. 'Sure, if you want to. I just have to make a phone call and then we'll hit the road.'

'OK.' Lucy waited till Uncle Reg was inside the house. 'Francis, are you there?'

He stepped out from the cover of a bush and shuffled uncertainly towards the truck. He looked warily at the other pigs. 'Do I know them?'

'Does it matter?' Lucy stood by the wide plank that led up, like steps, into the truck. 'Get on. We haven't got much time.'

'I just thought I should be introduced,' Francis protested. 'I don't know anyone.'

Lucy looked at Matilda and had a sudden burst of inspiration. 'Francis, I've got a surprise for you. This is your mum. Now, get on.'

'Did you say –?'

'Yes. Get on, will you?' Lucy pushed him gently.

'Oh ... all right.' He walked gingerly up the plank and paused at the gate.

'Francis, I have to shut it. Move!'

Lucy gave his bottom an almighty shove and, with a very pig-like squeal, he fell into the straw. 'What did you do that for?'

'Sorry.' Lucy tried to cheer him up. 'Look, this trip'll be a lot better than any book you've ever read. Believe me.'

Maybe she's right, Francis considered. This could be the adventure I've always wanted – once I get used to the truck and these strange pigs.

Matilda's snout poked out between the boards of the pen and she sniffed Francis. She recognised his smell. 'Hullo, Son,' she grunted pleasantly in pig language.

Francis went silent with shock.

'See, you're with family. She likes you.' Lucy smiled. 'Now, move over. I've got to get in too.'

15

ON THE ROAD

Francis felt the warm wind and the dust in his face, and sneezed.

'You OK?' Lucy asked.

'I'm hunky-dory, thanks.'

As the truck sped down the highway, Francis admired the farmhouses, the gum trees and the green paddocks stretching far into the distance. 'This is excellent. This is great! How far have we gone now?'

'About twenty k's.'

'Are we out of Makin Valley yet? What part of Australia are we in?' Francis was bursting with curiosity.

'Well, this is only a little bit of one state.

There are a lot of other places as well.'

'Yes, I understand that. Planet Earth: land surface, 149 million square kilometres; highest point, Mount Everest at 8,848 metres. I've –'

'Read about it,' Lucy cut in. 'I know.'

'Well, you don't really appreciate it till you see it,' he explained. 'The lakes and the birds. The grass and the trees. It's cool, really cool.'

Lucy hid her worries with a smile. She was pleased that Francis was enjoying the trip, but she hadn't thought their escape through. And he didn't even know it *was* an escape. Her only plan was to get him to the showgrounds and then to try to keep ahead of Dr Price.

Francis took his eyes off the passing countryside and glanced at Matilda feeding her piglets. 'Is she really my mother?'

'Uncle Reg reckons she is. They got the egg that made up you – from her.'

'I didn't think I had a mother,' Francis said gravely. 'I thought I was an orphan – like Oliver Twist. Excuse me a moment.'

He thought about what to say. 'Hullo, Mother, can I ask you a few questions about my ancestry?' he squeaked in pig tones.

'Leave me alone – can't you see I'm busy

with this lot!' Matilda replied in a high-pitched whine.

'Sorry ... Mum.'

'What was that all about?' Lucy asked.

'Sibling rivalry, I'm afraid.'

Lucy had never experienced it, but she'd often wondered what it would be like to have a brother or sister. Of course, that would be the ideal way of introducing Francis to people, she thought. 'Hi, this is my brother, Francis. He's the smart one in the family.' If only he wasn't a pig, Lucy thought.

She forgot the fantasy and reached for her lunch box. 'You want something to eat? Aunt Vittoria packed some food.'

'Yeah, I'm famished.' Francis eyed the food. 'Travel really makes you hungry.'

'Sandwich or an apple?'

'A sanger? I've never had a sanger,' Francis said animatedly. 'What's in it?'

'Cheese and tomato.'

'Sounds good.' Francis opened his mouth and Lucy fed him half the sandwich. He chewed it slowly, savouring the taste. 'Mm, it's piquant, isn't it?'

'I think it's cheddar.'

'The flavour – I read it in a dictionary. Piquant: sharp of taste and flavour,' he said. 'I've always wanted to use that word. It's definitely piquant.'

'If you say so.'

'Am I going to enjoy this show we're going to?'

'It's fantastic,' Lucy enthused. 'There are lots of other animals. And hot dogs and fairy floss and rides. And show bags. It's a blast.'

'A blast? Wowser!'

A blast meant good times ahead. Out in the world was absolutely the best place to be, Francis decided. He turned his face into the wind and practised his smile.

Vittoria stood on the verandah of the house and shrugged her shoulders. 'I'm sorry, Dr Price, but they've gone. They left two hours ago.'

'I'm afraid this is more serious than you think,' Amanda replied. 'I must speak to Lucy.'

'If you don't mind me asking, why?'

'I just wanted to check up on one of the pigs she's been feeding. It's important.'

'Well, they'll probably get to the show-grounds in about an hour. Reg usually rings me,' Vittoria said. 'Do you want me to ask him?'

'The showgrounds, of course.' Amanda moved off. 'I'll catch up with them there. Thank you, Vittoria.'

As she walked to her car, she quickly dialled a number on her mobile phone.

'Oh, hullo, Brian ... it's Amanda. We have a little crisis on our hands.'

The truck weaved its way through the busy city traffic and Francis tried not to sneeze again.

'Uh, uh ...' he snuffled. 'What's that awful smell?'

'Exhaust fumes,' Lucy explained. 'They cause a lot of pollution.'

'They're making my nose itchy,' Francis complained. The big skyscrapers, the wide streets and the thousands and thousands of people were amazing; but if this was the city, he was pretty sure he didn't like it. 'Why are there all these cars? Where do they go?'

'To work, the shops, everywhere,' Lucy replied. 'Everyone in the city has a car.'

At the lights, Reg leaned out of the window and shouted at Lucy. 'How's it going back there?'

'OK, Uncle Reg.'

'We'll be there in five minutes. The pigs all right?'

'They're great,' Lucy replied, standing in front of Francis so Uncle Reg couldn't see him.

The lights changed and the truck lurched off. Lucy gripped the wire mesh screening and watched the buildings go by. They passed the Children's Hospital, and she thought guiltily of Henry Price. He's in there, waiting for his operation, and I'm escaping with the only creature who can save him. But she knew she couldn't let Francis down. He was just as intelligent as Henry and had just as much right to live.

16
BOXED IN

People were queuing up at the turnstiles as Reg showed his pass and drove slowly through the giant arch of the showground gates.

'They'll open to the public in about ten minutes,' he called back to Lucy. 'With this warm weather, there'll be a big turnout.'

The truck's engine grated into lower gear and Reg drove at a snail's pace through the grounds. Hundreds of stall-holders rushed about, getting ready to sell everything from burgers and drinks to toys and farm machinery.

A farmer in a tweed jacket and moleskin trousers at the roadside called out to Reg. 'G'day, mate, good to see ya.'

'G'day, Tom!' Reg turned into another road lined with poles and coloured flags flapping in the strong morning breeze. The truck moved past the main oval and headed towards the huge animal pavilions in the distance.

'This is gigantic,' Francis said. 'Is this all one show?'

'Yep.'

'How long does it last?'

'About ten days.' Lucy looked down the long, empty avenues. She loved the feeling of arriving early, before the crowds flocked in and the rubbish started to pile up. And before the endless recorded announcements started from the food trailers – 'Roasting, toasting all the time! Hot chickens and toasted sandwiches! The only percolated coffee on the showgrounds!' She knew them all off by heart.

The truck swayed as Reg took a hard turn to the right. 'Where are we going now?' Francis asked anxiously.

'Ssh, Uncle Reg will hear you.'

The truck pulled up at the back entrance to the pig pavilion and stopped. Lucy jumped out.

'Francis, keep out of sight and don't move.'

Francis wriggled his snout from under a pile of straw. 'How long do I have to stay in here?'

'Not long.'

The driver's door slammed shut and Reg came around to the rear of the truck. 'Gees, Lucy, what on earth were you blabbing about? Thought you'd never shut up on the drive down.'

'Um, I was ...' Lucy searched for an excuse. 'I was learning a poem ... for school.'

'You've got to stop talking to yourself.' He grinned and tapped the side of his head. 'Madness. Next it'll be hairs on the palms of your hands.'

Lucy stood between Uncle Reg and the back gate of the truck. 'I'll unload the pigs, if you want to call Aunt Vittoria.'

'Righto. I'll let her know we got here in one piece.' He made for the office at the end of the building. 'We'll be in the same place as last year, Luce. Back in a minute!'

When he was out of sight, Lucy unbolted the gate and fixed the plank into place. 'Francis – out! And follow me.'

'I'm coming, I'm coming.' He wobbled down

the plank on unsteady legs. When he reached the ground, Lucy slipped the loop of a rope around his neck.

'What's with the leash?' he complained. 'What do you think I am – a pooch?'

On entering the showgrounds, Lucy had remembered the sleeping boxes at the end of the pig pavilion. Each farmer had a small locked room, about three metres square, where they could stay while their pigs were on show.

'Down this way.' Lucy led Francis through the long rows of wooden-railed pens. Dozens of animals had already arrived from all over the state. The air was filled with their rhythmic grunts and the building reeked strongly from their smell. Lucy could spot the different breeds – the reddish-brown Durocs, the black Berkshires, the black-and-white Hampshires and the Large Whites and Landraces like Francis. In a few of the pens, farmers were busily brushing their pigs down, grooming them for the judging ring tomorrow.

'Not so fast!' Francis groaned, trying to keep up. 'And why is this all such a big secret?'

Lucy ignored him and didn't slow down till they reached the sleeping boxes. Uncle Reg's name – REG MARLOW – was chalked on one of the doors. 'In here, quick.'

She dragged Francis inside and unhooked the rope from his neck. The room was roughly furnished with a couple of single beds and a wardrobe, and had a hand basin in one corner.

'I hate to bring up such a delicate matter as personal hygiene,' Francis said impatiently, 'but pigs can't sweat to regulate body temperature. And I'm getting thirsty.'

Lucy put the plug in the basin and turned on the tap. 'If you need some water, drink this.' She headed for the door. 'And whatever you do, don't leave. And keep quiet. Please.'

'Where are you going?' Francis asked unhappily. 'And why do I have to stay –?'

'I can't talk now,' Lucy interrupted. 'I have to help Uncle Reg. Be back soon.'

'When's lunch?' Being out in the big world, Francis had discovered, gave you a humungous appetite.

'When we get round to it.'

Instead of going through the pavilion, Lucy strolled into the open air and took the long way round to the truck. She could hear the music from the Ferris wheel in the distance, and now the gates were open, groups of people had begun to wander through the showgrounds. Lucy ignored them and tried to work out what to do next. She had to find a safe place to hide Francis for a while.

Up ahead, Lucy spotted Uncle Reg by the truck, arguing with a man. It was Brian, one of the businessmen Dr Price knew. The big man with the red hair and beard.

Reg saw Lucy and called out. 'Lucy, what's this about Francis? Where is he?'

Lucy froze and Brian spun round. 'Stay there, young lady! Whatever you do – don't move!'

17
OFF THE LEASH

'What's Fairy Floss?' Francis took an interest in all the signs. 'Is it like dental floss?'

'No, it's not.' Lucy glanced nervously at the faces in the crowd and fought the urge to break into a run – that would attract even more attention. As it was, the sight of a pig on a leash had people nudging one another and saying, 'Oh, look. Isn't that cute?'

'See, even they think I'm a mutt,' Francis complained.

'Ssh, don't talk!' Lucy whispered forcefully. 'People will stare even more if you do.'

'I can bark if you like.'

As they got closer to the main exit, Lucy saw

flashing lights. Two police cars were parked across the roadway and four policemen stood nearby with Brian. He must know some important people, Lucy thought. In the five minutes since she'd taken Francis from the sleeping box, he'd got police patrols to watch for anyone leaving the showgrounds. She dragged Francis to a halt.

'Hey, you're choking me,' he protested.

'Let's go this way.' She steered him towards a lane at the back of the oval.

'There she is – that's them!' Brian called out. 'Come on!'

Lucy gathered in the rope. 'Francis – trust me – and run!'

Francis was caught off guard. His short stumpy legs scrambled frantically as he tried to keep up with her. 'Why – why run?'

'For the exercise!'

On her last five visits to the Show, Lucy had thoroughly explored the showgrounds and knew that there were six exits. The nearest one was on the other side of the oval and she headed that way, dodging through a line of cows on their way to the dairy pavilion.

'Hey, watch where you're going!' a red-faced farmer complained, as he tried to stop a heifer bucking.

'Sorry!' Lucy veered to the right through a small gate and ran onto the oval. Scores of ponies and their young riders were jumping, or waiting to jump, over a complicated course of rails and hurdles. A hundred metres away, two policemen appeared in front of the grandstand and pointed in her direction. Lucy sized up the situation. 'We've got to get away from here.'

The only way was through the course. A pony and rider jumped over the rail ahead and Lucy followed them.

'Jump, Francis!'

'Unnnh!' Francis groaned as he landed heavily on the other side.

'Keep running!'

Behind them, the two policemen weaved their way through a group of ponies and riders and jumped over three hurdles in a row. A wave of applause and laughter swept through the crowd.

'And ladies and gentlemen,' the announcer called over the public address system, 'it seems we have a novelty event today. A pig chased by pigs!'

As a round of cheering broke out, Lucy and Francis avoided two ponies and made for a grey-coated official guarding a gate. Lucy heard the crowd scream with delight and she glanced back. One policeman had tripped over a rail and splashed head first into the water hazard. He struggled to his feet, the muddy water dripping from his uniform.

'One down, ladies and gentlemen, and one to go!' The announcer's voice boomed around the ground.

'Stop, stop there!' The grey-coated man tried to block Lucy from reaching the gate.

'Maybe ... we ... should ... stop,' Francis puffed.

'Not yet!'

Lucy let the rope trail along the ground between her and Francis, and when the man got closer, pulled it tight and tripped him up. A thunder of applause echoed around the oval.

'And the pig wins!' the announcer said. 'Put your hands together everyone; a big round of applause!'

Outside the oval, Francis stopped. 'I ... have ... to get my breath.' He gasped a few times and looked seriously at Lucy. 'Dr Price doesn't know about this trip to the Show, does she?'

'No. I just said that to get you away.'

'I want to talk. I want to know what's really going on.'

'We'll find somewhere to hide,' Lucy tugged vigorously at the rope. 'Just a bit further.'

'But what's it all about?' Vittoria's voice came down the line. 'And where is Lucy exactly?'

'I don't know,' Reg answered with concern. 'She could be anywhere.'

'But why did Lucy take Francis away from the farm?'

'Beats me,' Reg replied, looking back along the line of impatient people waiting to use the public phone. He smiled, trying to indicate he wouldn't be long. 'One of those blokes who knows Dr Price is here – reckons Lucy has stolen him because he's worth a lot. What's the doc say about it?'

'Not much,' Vittoria said. 'Anyway, she left for the city over an hour ago. You'll probably see her this afternoon. And she's pretty mad.'

'Great, I can hardly wait.'

'... And that's basically what I found out. That's why I wanted to get you out of the laboratory.'

With the ponies out on the oval, the stables were empty and quiet. Lucy had found a stall far away from the door and told Francis everything she knew.

Thoughtfully, Francis nestled his head on a pile of sweet-smelling straw. He'd always imagined the pigs that were taken away went to some wonderful, sunny, Genius Genes Corporation farm. A place with green rolling hills, comfortable pens and plenty of food. And nights of looking up at the bright, twinkling stars. That they were being raised for transplant experiments shocked him deeply. 'So, the pigs all die in the end?'

'I think so,' Lucy said sadly. 'As far as I know, anyway.'

'And Dr Price wants to do the same to me?'

'Sort of ... only she wants to do a real operation. This transplant with your brain.'

'And have you met Henry?'

'Yes.'

'And part of me, genes from his body, were used to make up my brain and other parts of me?'

'That's what Dr Price reckons.'

'So, in a way, Henry and I are related.' Francis scratched his nose with his left trotter. It was little comfort, but at least he knew all the facts. 'Will you do something for me, Lucy?'

'Sure.'

'Take me to see Henry.'

'You're kidding?' Lucy said. 'He's in the hospital. It'll be pretty hard.'

'I know,' Francis replied. 'But I really want to see him.'

18
A WAY OUT?

The tall, uniformed police sergeant walked up to Brian. 'We've got officers covering all the exits, Mr Martin.'

'What about inside the showgrounds?' he asked.

'A dozen officers are searching all the buildings,' the sergeant answered. 'But it'll take a while for them to report back.'

'I needn't remind you, this pig is very valuable,' Brian said tersely. 'And I don't want any mistakes. I want him back.'

At the side of the dog pavilion, Lucy found a

metal rubbish bin, climbed onto it and peered over a wooden fence.

Ten metres away, two policemen stood guard at an exit and she could hear the occasional crackle of voices on their radios. She looked down at Francis. 'No luck here either, they're all covered.' In the last half hour they'd checked every gate.

'How are we going to get away?'

Lucy jumped off the bin. 'It's gonna be hard.' The trouble is keeping out of sight, she thought. The hospital was about ten minutes away, once they were through the gates. But that was the big problem – getting out. 'Let's take another look around.'

Francis didn't mind Lucy tugging on the rope now, and trotted patiently alongside. Lucy kicked her way through some rubbish and old newspapers at the back of the pavilion and stopped at the next corner.

She peered cautiously into Machinery Square, where the manufacturers displayed their tractors, harvesters and other agricultural equipment. In a demonstration area, a small crowd of farmers watched a bright-blue tractor snake its way through a line of barrels. At the end of the line, the tractor turned sharply in front of the high brick wall that circled the entire showgrounds. The skilful display of steering brought applause from the farmers and the driver decided to tackle the course again.

Lucy's face brightened. She'd often watched Uncle Reg driving his tractor and knew that they were bulky and hard to steer. 'Francis, I've got an idea.'

Francis peeked around her legs. 'You want to steal the tractor?'

'Better than that. Follow me.'

Francis stuck close to Lucy's side as they skirted round the farmers. The tractor was halfway down the course and Lucy watched its progress intently.

'Francis, if the tractor turns and comes back again, do exactly as I say.'

'OK.'

As she had hoped, more clapping from the group encouraged the driver to take another spin. Lucy led Francis to the point where the tractor would have to turn very close to the brick wall. 'When I say so, run right at the front of the tractor,' she ordered.

'What?' Francis squeaked.

'You want to see Henry?'

'Sure.'

'Then just do it. Please.'

This is going to take split-second timing, Lucy calculated. The tractor threaded its way through the barrels, reached the last one and then began to circle back. 'Now! Now!' she shouted.

Francis sucked in a deep breath and charged at the tractor. The driver could hardly believe his eyes. He gave the horn a mighty blast, and with a flurry of hands on the wheel, swerved away from Francis. The tractor ploughed into the brick wall and tore out a huge hole.

Francis stopped in his tracks and stared in amazement.

'Step on it – this way!' Lucy yelled, as she dragged Francis towards the gap in the wall. They clambered over the pile of broken bricks and made it to the street on the other side.

From somewhere nearby, Lucy heard the wail of a police siren. 'Hate to say it, Franky – but run!'

In the pig pavilion, Reg filled up Matilda's trough, gave her a pat and moved around Brian Martin and the police sergeant.

'Are you sure you can't tell us where Lucy is likely to go?' Brian demanded.

'I'm sorry, fellas, I can't help you.' Reg forked a pile of fresh straw into the stall holding his champion boar. He fixed his eyes on the sergeant. 'Can't you put out one of those radio reports, an all-points-bulletin, or whatever you call them?'

'We've got a full squad searching for her now,' the policeman replied. 'A photo of her would help – you got one, Mr Marlow?'

Reg reached into his back pocket and opened his wallet. 'This is Lucy – with my wife.' He handed the policeman a crumpled photograph.

'Thanks. Gives us a better chance of finding her.' The man looked apologetically at Brian. 'And the pig, of course.'

'I want to find Lucy, too,' Reg said honestly. 'No good having kids wandering about these days. Never know what might happen.'

Brian remained unconvinced. He poked Reg in the chest and said, 'Look, we've given you plenty of business and a lot of money over the last year! I'd hate to think you were holding out on us. It wouldn't be good for you!'

This annoyed Reg and the anger rose in his throat. However, his reply was prevented by the arrival of a policewoman.

'Sergeant, they've been spotted. They've got out of the showgrounds,' she said.

'Damn it!' Brian grabbed the sergeant by the arm and turned swiftly on his heels. 'Come on, man, move it!'

Reg was glad to see them go. He didn't like being threatened by a creep like Brian Martin. If it came to taking sides, his loyalties lay with Lucy and that pig, Francis. The pig that everyone seemed to want. Why was everyone carrying on about him? he wondered.

Now that he was actually in the world, Francis was unsure about it. In the laboratory, the outside world had seemed a magical, fascinating place. In reality, it was turning into a nightmare. It was full of traffic, crowds, people in blue uniforms who wanted to chase him – and doctors who wanted his brain.

'Are we nearly there?' he asked Lucy anxiously.

'Up around the next corner.' Lucy tried to work out how they'd get into the hospital. She'd have heaps of trouble convincing the security guards she had to visit Henry with a pet pig.

'Hold it!' Lucy saw red flashing lights up ahead and dragged Francis into a shop entrance.

A moment later, she sneaked a quick look and saw an ambulance parked up the street. A bent and broken bicycle lay in the roadway and two ambulancemen were lifting someone on a stretcher into the back of the vehicle.

'What are you doing, if I may ask?' a voice said behind her.

Lucy turned into the fierce gaze of a young woman standing in the door of the shop. 'Sorry, just window-shopping.'

'Really – see anything your size?' The woman asked.

Lucy checked out the window. It was full of mannequins wearing coloured bras and pants. 'It's him.' She smiled apologetically at Francis. 'He likes women's underwear.'

'Do I?' Francis asked innocently.

'Bye!' Lucy moved out onto the pavement again.

'Stick with me, Francis, and take it slowly.' She kept an eye on the ambulancemen as they made their patient comfortable. They stepped out, shut the back doors of the ambulance, and moved to the front cabin. 'There's our chance. Follow me!'

Lucy ran to the ambulance, and as the engine started, she grabbed the handle and opened the doors. 'Get in, get in!'

Francis leapt into the ambulance and Lucy scrambled in after him.

As they moved into the traffic, Francis stared at the young man with a bandaged head lying on the stretcher. He reached out and touched Francis on the leg. 'Doctor, I can't see too well. Am I going to be all right?' he croaked.

Lucy nudged Francis and whispered, 'Say something.'

Francis curled his sensitive nose around the man's wrist and felt his pulse. It seemed strong and healthy.

'Yep, you'll be fine.'

'Thanks, Doc.' The man breathed a sigh of relief.

19
BROTHERS

The hospital reminded Lucy of the laboratory at the farm. It had the same sort of smell and atmosphere. The big difference was the grey-tiled walls that seemed to go on forever.

'We have to get up to the next floor,' Lucy whispered.

'Why are you talking so quietly?' Francis said. 'There's no-one around.'

'I dunno. You always whisper in hospitals,' Lucy said. 'Can you walk up stairs?'

'I guess so.'

'We better use them,' Lucy said. 'It's nearly visiting time and people might be in the lifts.'

She saw the stairwell up ahead and heard

voices nearby. She touched Francis gently on the head, put her finger to her lips and they crept forward.

Francis walked on tiptoe, trying to stop his trotters clacking loudly on the floor.

The first door on the right was open and a lot of loud voices echoed strangely in the room.

Lucy craned her neck around the doorway. A TV set was on and a little girl was sitting up in bed, flicking from channel to channel with a remote control. 'Hi,' she said, looking straight at Lucy. 'What do you wanna watch?'

'Nothing at the moment, thanks,' Lucy replied. 'Francis, that's TV. The real thing.'

Francis stared at the images. Two large bananas were talking and dancing in a forest of coloured cardboard trees. 'That's TV – dancing bananas?'

'It gets better later in the day.'

'I'll take your word for it.'

The girl pointed the remote at Francis and clicked it again and again. 'Go away. I don't like talking pigs; go away.'

'Oh, you prefer listening to fruit?' Francis said.

'Go away!' She clicked the remote again.

'She's right.' Lucy led him away. Upstairs, the

second floor was busier. Doctors, nurses and orderlies bustled to and fro.

'This doesn't look easy,' Francis said from behind a basketful of dirty laundry. 'Where's Henry's room?'

'Down there,' Lucy indicated. 'Let's wait a minute.'

A nurse and a doctor chatted for a few seconds and then moved on. The corridor was clear.

'Now's our chance.' Lucy held the rope firmly in her hand, ready to escape at any moment. But they reached Henry's room without incident and Lucy peeked in. Dr Price and another doctor were talking by Henry's bed. She must have just arrived from the farm, Lucy thought. And she looks upset. Henry lay unconscious and was connected to a lot of tubes and a machine that beeped and showed fuzzy green lines on a small screen.

Lucy spotted a curtain around the empty bed nearest the door and nudged Francis. They quickly ducked behind it. Lucy moved around to the other side of the bed and listened.

'I was just on the phone,' Amanda told the other doctor. 'Francis has completely disappeared. If we can't find him, what are we going to do, Ross?'

Lucy thought about the name for a few seconds and then made the connection. He was Henry's father, the brain surgeon.

'Well, we've only got a few days,' he answered tightly. 'We can keep Henry on the machine and keep him alive. After that ...'

There was silence between the couple. The only sound in the room was the beeping of the machine.

'After that, it's just luck if he lives,' Amanda said painfully. 'I better talk to Brian and see how the search is going. It's our only hope.'

Lucy waited impatiently as they left Henry's bedside and walked across the floor and out of the room.

'Can I see him now?' Francis asked.

Lucy opened the curtain and they approached Henry's bed. His right arm was outside the covers and Francis stepped closer and sniffed it.

'He doesn't smell ... well,' Francis reported.

'I think he's really sick. He's ...'

'He's dying, yes.' His nose moved up Henry's body and reached his bald head. 'Poor kiddo.' Like a friendly dog, he flicked out his tongue and licked him. 'How old is he?'

'About the same age as you. Eleven – in human years,' Lucy added.

'We're like brothers when you think about it,' Francis murmured. 'I'm part of him and he's part of me.'

Lucy left them together and walked away from the bed. All she could think about was hiding Francis. But where?

On the bedside table, she noticed a photo of Henry and his dad at the beach wearing flippers and snorkels. The beach! Why hadn't she thought of that before?

'Francis, we'll be in trouble if we hang around the hospital much longer. And I've got a plan. A real plan.'

Francis looked at her curiously and sneezed – a loud one that set his whole body wobbling.

'Are you all right?' Lucy asked anxiously.

He sneezed again. 'Uh ... uh ... I think I'm getting a cold.'

Reg munched a few potato wedges and handed the bag to Vittoria. 'There's a few left, want some?'

'No thanks.' Vittoria had lost her appetite

since coming down to the showgrounds on the train. She wanted to be around while the police looked for Lucy.

'Did Bob Jones mind feeding the pigs?' Reg asked between mouthfuls.

'No, he's happy to do it for as long as we're away.' Vittoria took Reg's hand. 'Does anybody know why Lucy's done this – exactly?'

'I don't know what's behind it. But she's a sensible kid, I'm sure she's got a good reason.'

'What possible reason could she have?'

He shrugged. 'Look, all I know is, she took one look at Brian and scarpered. And I don't blame her. There's something a bit strange about that guy, and why he wants Francis so bad.'

'So, what do we do?'

'We wait.' Reg squeezed her hand. 'If Lucy needs us, she'll be in touch.'

Lucy got out her purse and counted her money – forty-two dollars in notes and coins. She put the old coat, the red woollen scarf and the wide-brimmed bush hat on the counter. 'I'll take these, thanks.'

The cheerful, white-haired lady scratched a

few numbers on a notepad with a pencil. 'That's ten dollars. Shall I wrap them for you?'

'No, it's OK. Thanks.'

Lucy bundled up the clothes and left the op shop. Outside, she calculated there was enough money left to buy bus tickets and food for a few days. She hurried down the street to the bus station.

In the big parking bay, two buses were loading. Lucy pushed her way through the long queues of passengers to the Departures Board, which showed that the bus for Shelly Beach would leave in half an hour.

She ducked behind two large bins at the side of the building. 'Francis, I'm back!'

He wasn't there.

'Francis? Francis?!' she gasped in a panicky voice.

There was a scuffling sound from under one of the bins and then a dusty snout appeared. 'What took you so long?'

'What are you doing under there?'

'A man came out and dumped rubbish. I thought I'd better hide.' Francis sneezed violently.

'You OK?'

'My n-nose is a bit r-runny,' he moaned.

'Look, I got you these. They'll keep you warm.'

Lucy wrapped the scarf round his neck and draped the coat over his back and buttoned it. 'How's that?'

'Fine,' he sniffled. 'But why are we hanging round here?'

'Mum and Dad have a holiday house at Shelly Beach. No-one's there at the moment, so we can hide for a while. As soon as the bus arrives, we'll get on board.'

20
COOLING IT

Lucy watched the bus pull into the parking bay. If her plan was going to work, they had to get on before anyone saw them. Fortunately, all the other buses and passengers had left. After a minute, the door of the bus whooshed open and the driver stepped out, yawned and strolled lazily towards the ticket office.

'You ready?'

Francis nodded and Lucy stepped out into the open.

She kept the bus between them and the windows of the terminal to reduce the chances of being seen. As they reached the bus, she checked the sign above the front window. It showed SHELLY BEACH. 'This is it, get in!'

Francis waddled up the steps, the long coat dragging around his legs. 'Where do I go?'

'Right down the back. As far from the door as possible.'

Ten minutes later, when the driver returned, they were settled into the furthest and darkest corner of the bus. The driver took off his sunglasses and glanced down the aisle at Lucy. 'Hey, is someone there?'

Lucy grabbed the hat and reached over to Francis.

'Keep this on your head.' She bent the wide brim over his snout and hid his face.

'It's just us.' Lucy stood and came forward with their tickets. 'My friend's got a bit of a cold, I didn't want to wait outside.'

The driver checked the tickets. 'That's OK. Should be leaving in a few minutes.'

'Thanks.' Lucy slid back into her seat and Francis sucked in a deep breath and sneezed.

'I ... fink ... uts ... getting worse,' he mumbled.

As Lucy tightened the scarf round his neck, she remembered what Dr Price had said about the risk of the pigs picking up germs. Francis must have got some sort of infection since he'd left the laboratory. 'Don't worry,' Lucy reassured him. 'We'll get you to bed as soon as we can.'

Francis closed his eyes and tried to rest. Lucy glanced out the window and almost jumped from the seat when she saw a police car pull up. Two officers got out and surveyed the bus terminal suspiciously.

'Francis, keep your head down,' Lucy said. 'Don't look outside.'

Francis stared at the floor and fought back a massive sneeze. Start the bus soon, Lucy prayed, please start it soon. The policemen began talking to the people in the queue and showing them a photo. One after another, the passengers shook their heads.

'Morning, dear.' A tiny, middle-aged woman wearing a black beret smiled cheerfully at Lucy and sat one seat up from the back and across the aisle.

'Hi,' Lucy replied.

'You and your friend going to Shelly Beach?' the woman asked.

Lucy didn't want to give any clues to their destination. 'Just out sight-seeing.'

'Lovely day for it.'

The engine roared to life and its powerful vibrations rattled down the length of the bus. Please, let's go, Lucy wished fervently. Let's get away from here.

'I'm not very happy.' Brian Martin glared at Amanda Price and stirred another two teaspoons of sugar into his coffee. 'Letting one of our pigs get away is inexcusable. They're worth over a hundred thousand dollars each.'

'I let you know as soon as I found out,' she apologised. She looked around the hospital cafe and hoped that no-one had overheard them. 'It was totally unexpected.'

'But that's only half of it. This Lucy, an inexperienced child, shouldn't have been let near those pigs,' he asserted. 'And I don't think you've been honest with us.'

'What do you mean?'

'I don't normally check your research records, but from what I can gather, this pig is pretty unusual, isn't he? *Francis*, I think you call him.'

'How do you know that name?'

'I sent security guards to the farm this afternoon and they've already reported to me,' Brian said. 'They're keeping a special watch on the pigs from now on.'

'That's not necessary –'

'What's necessary is that we get *our* Francis back,' he interrupted. 'I know you've put a lot of work into him and that he has special genetic material in his body. You're keeping something from us, I think, something that might make us even more money.'

'There's nothing special about him, really,' Amanda lied.

'Oh yes there is.' Brian slammed his cup down on the table. 'And I intend to get him back and find out what it is.'

In the hot afternoon sun, the bus moved onto the southern freeway. Lucy heard only two sounds – the whistling of the wind past the windows and Francis sniffling from his cold. A tremendous sneeze racked his body and his hat nearly fell off.

'Oh, bless you!' the woman in the seat nearby exclaimed. 'Would your friend like a lozenge? They're menthol.'

'Thank you.' Lucy took the sweet and held it

in the palm of her hand. 'Try this, Frank, it's just the thing for your cold.'

'Ah, ah ...' Francis tried to stop sneezing.

'Open wide,' Lucy said.

Francis slipped out his tongue and took the lozenge. It rolled around his mouth, tasted sweet for a second and then started to burn his throat. 'P-too! Pah!' He spat the lozenge across the bus and it splattered against the window in front of the woman. 'Yuggh, it's awful! What's that poison?'

'Well, I'm sorry.' The woman turned away in a huff. 'There's no pleasing some people.'

'Just cool it, Francis,' Lucy said soothingly. 'Cool it, please.'

21
SAND AND SPAGHETTI

'Is this where you want to get out?' the driver asked.

In the darkness, the bus slowed down along the road north of Shelly Beach.

Lucy scanned the nearby bush and houses over the driver's shoulder. 'This is it, thanks.'

'You sure you'll be OK?'

'Yeah. Mum and Dad's house is just down by the beach.' That was true, but she didn't want to tell him it was over a kilometre away and far from the other houses. Or that her parents were in Italy. The less anyone knew, the better. 'I'll wake up my friend.'

'Okey-doke.' The driver stopped the bus

and pulled on the handbrake.

Back at her seat, Lucy woke Francis. 'Look, there's no other way of doing this. We'll just have to walk out through the front.'

'Won't people see me? Won't –?'

'Don't worry, we'll just act real casual.'

Francis struggled out of the seat and his feet thudded onto the floor. Lucy glanced at the woman nearby and was relieved to see she was asleep. 'You go first.'

Francis walked to the front door. 'Thanks, driver ... ah ... it was a blast.' He sneezed loudly. 'And so was that.'

'Bless you, sir.' The driver looked across and watched Francis step down from the bus. He shook his head in disbelief and turned to Lucy. 'Was that a pig in a raincoat?'

'Sure, any problem with that?'

The man scratched his bald head. 'Young lady, when you've been driving a bus as long as I have, nothing's a problem.'

Lucy jumped down the step. 'Thanks. Bye.'

'Ahh ... choo!' Francis sneezed in the cool night air.

'Take it easy.' The driver closed the door and, with a pulsating roar, the bus accelerated down the road. In the half moonlight, Lucy tried to make out the dirt track to the beach house. She didn't notice the woman in the black beret staring down angrily at them from her seat on the bus.

'Come on, Francis.' Lucy hitched the rope around his neck. 'We've got a bit of a hike.

Francis downed the last of the hot lemon drink, took a deep, sniffly breath through his nostrils, and lay his head back down on the pillow. 'That was very good. Is it your own concoction?'

Lucy put the mug on the living room table and unfolded a blanket. 'It's Grandma Rosalba's cure-all for colds. Fresh lemon juice, honey, cloves, ginger and hot water. Just relax and let it work.'

Francis stretched out on the couch and Lucy covered him with the blanket. 'That OK?'

'Fine, thanks.' He felt more comfortable than he'd ever been in the laboratory. Beds or couches should be a part of every pig's life, he decided. And no pig should ever sleep without a blanket.

Lucy knelt by the couch and stroked his right

ear. 'You're more Large White than Landrace, you know.'

'How do you know?'

'Landrace pigs have floppy ears and Large Whites have ears that stand up,' she replied. 'Yours stand up. You probably have more Large White genes.'

'And more human genes than any pig,' Francis added seriously.

'True. The most human pig of all time.'

Francis looked at Lucy curiously. 'Would you say we've become friends now?'

'Sure. I reckon.'

'I always thought it would be hard to make friends,' Francis went on. 'That it took years and there were many trials and tribulations. That you had to share many adventures and many experiences before learning the true value of friendship. In books, that happens all the time.'

'We've had a lot of adventures in a short time,' Lucy said 'Maybe that makes you friends quicker.'

Francis lifted his head and licked Lucy's cheek gently. 'We're friends. Whatever happens, we'll always be friends.'

Lucy rested her head next to his and

listened to the sound of the waves outside.

'There is one thing, though,' Francis said abruptly.

In a panic, Lucy sat up. 'What?'

'Can we light a fire on the beach and cook spaghetti? I've never eaten spaghetti and I've heard it's pretty ace.'

Lucy relaxed. 'Yeah, we can eat spaghetti. Alla funghi. With mushrooms.'

'That would be absolutely far out.' Francis wriggled down into the blanket. 'Night ... dag.'

'Night ... piggy.'

22
A PIG IS A PIG?

'So, you're telling me Francis is one of these transgenic pigs,' Reg stated.

'Yes, the best I've ever produced,' Amanda replied with a hint of pride.

'I read about them once,' Reg said. 'They started breeding these pigs at Cambridge University didn't they? In England.'

'Yes, they were the first to see their potential for organ donation. I visited there a few years ago.'

'I thought you were just doing breeding experiments, Doc.' Reg appraised her suspiciously. 'You know, leaner pigs with less fat and all that.'

'I probably said something like that when we built the laboratory. I'm sorry, but we wanted to keep our work secret.'

Reg walked a few paces to the back door of the pig pavilion. The sun was rising over the Ferris wheel and roosters crowed from the direction of the poultry exhibits. Last night, Dr Price had sent a message asking Reg to meet her alone. He'd only agreed in the hope of picking up more information about Lucy – and Francis. Now, he was almost sorry he'd asked about the pig. 'You're not serious about this brain transplant, are you?'

'Theoretically, there's no organ you can't transplant,' Amanda said. 'With the brain it's more complicated, because you have to rejoin the nerve cells between the brain and the spinal cord. The operation will take many, many hours. But Ross and I have also developed a special nerve growth chemical that we think will help the rejoining process.'

'And your son will have another brain – just like his?'

'That's why I created Francis in this way,' Amanda explained. 'A brain exactly the same.'

'Well, the only thing you didn't count on was Lucy.'

'You're partly responsible for that too,' she said accusingly. 'You recommended her.'

'Oh, I see,' Reg smiled knowingly. 'This meeting's all about blaming me –'

'Perhaps taking responsibility for Lucy's actions. And helping me get Francis back.'

'I don't blame Lucy, you know,' Reg said bluntly. 'That might sound funny from a bloke who breeds pigs for the pork and bacon trade. But my pigs – they're real pigs – if you get what I mean. They're not pigs with human body bits. The whole idea makes me sick.'

'Science always has to go forwards,' Amanda responded. 'And sometimes, scientists have to go into unpopular areas. We have to do things that people might disapprove of.'

'Oh, yeah. I'd like to know why.'

'In my case, because of Henry. I love him and I want to try to save his life. But I might have easily bred Francis just to see if it could be done. That would interest me too.' She rose from her seat on a hay bale and joined Reg at the door. 'This still doesn't help us find Lucy, or Francis. We could get this trouble over very quickly.'

'The only trouble ... is being caused by your

bossy mate, Brian,' Reg replied.

'Forget him. We can work this out ourselves.'

'You still think I know where she is, don't you?'

'Yes.'

'Well, honestly, I don't,' Reg said forcefully. 'Look, my position is this. Lucy's the only one who's had the guts to do anything about this situation. And I reckon she knows what she's doing. I think she's OK.'

'I hope, for your sake, you're right,' Amanda said.

Francis slept. In his dream, his ears were much bigger than normal and were flapping like Dumbo the Elephant's. As he flew over the ocean towards the Sydney Opera House, he heard a voice calling from far below. 'I'm down here, I'm down here,' it was saying.

He flapped his left ear faster and changed direction towards the sound. A long, white beach stretched far into the horizon and hundreds of brown seals basked in the sunshine. But they made no sound. 'Over here, over here!' the voice kept calling.

Francis wheeled around and glided back

along the beach. A big, bull seal bellowed a loud roar at the sky and, for a moment, drowned out the voice. On a rocky outcrop pounded by huge waves, someone waved a white piece of cloth. 'Can you see me? Can you see me?' the person called.

Francis glided in closer and the figure looked up at him. It was Henry Price. He'd taken the white bandage from his head and was whirling it round and round in the air. He waved at Francis and fell head first into the sea. The waves crashed onto the rocks and Henry sank underwater. His arm rose, holding the bandage, and then slipped underwater again. Francis called back, 'I'm coming! I'm coming!'

He woke with a shock and tumbled off the couch.

The sun shone through the windows and, in front of the house, he saw the rocky cliff and the pathway that led about twenty metres down to a quiet stretch of beach. Gentle waves washed up onto the sand. It was early and there were no swimmers or surfers in sight. Francis pushed open the screen door with his snout and stepped onto the deck. He sniffed the wind and noticed a familiar smell.

He clambered down the steps and sniffed the breeze again. The smell came from inland and he headed off in that direction, away from the sea.

In the pig pavilion, Vittoria stood close to Reg, trying to listen in on his phone conversation.

'Are you all right, Lucy?' Reg asked.

Yes, I'm OK,' Lucy's voice crackled down the line. 'It's Francis, I can't find him.'

'Look, where are you?'

'I better not say,' Lucy said tensely. 'We got here last night and he went to sleep. Then this morning he was gone.'

'Can we do anything to help her?' Vittoria butted in.

'I heard that,' Lucy replied. 'Tell Aunt Vittoria I'm OK. I've got food and stuff.'

Reg nodded reassuringly at Vittoria and spoke into the phone. 'Lucy, give us a ring tomorrow. I know why you've done this, love, and it's OK. If you need any help, just call me.'

'Thanks, I will. Bye!'

Reg hung up and gave Vittoria a hug. 'Told you she'd be all right.'

Up in the top floor office of the grandstand, about four hundred metres away, a policeman switched off a tape-recorder and some fancy electronic equipment. He took off his headphones and dialled a number on his mobile phone. 'Hullo, Mr Martin? ... That woman who complained to us about the girl and the pig was right. I've traced them to a phone at Shelly Beach.'

23
EATING ELSEWHERE

Lucy threw another driftwood branch onto the fire. It cast a golden glow over the small cove and private beach, just down from the house. In the middle of the blaze, water boiled in a metal pot, waiting for the spaghetti. A frypan gently bubbled with the cream and mushroom sauce – the exact recipe that Aunt Vittoria made.

All day, Lucy had tried not to panic. She'd bought the food and rung Uncle Reg from the Shelly Beach General Store. Wherever Francis had gone, she thought, surely he wouldn't miss his first ever spaghetti dinner.

'Ohh!' Lucy was startled as a lone seagull screeched and flew over the waves towards the sunset. Earlier this afternoon, she'd taken Dad's old binoculars and walked to the top of the big sand dunes, half a kilometre away. From there, you could see the town, the carpark and the whole beach – north and south. If Francis was around, she figured she'd see him from there.

Once, she saw a police car pull up at the Surf Lifesaving Club. A policeman and woman had gone inside for about half an hour. Later, they'd walked up and down the whole length of the beach. After a couple of hours, and no sign of Francis, Lucy had given up, and began collecting wood for the fire.

A sizzling sound brought Lucy's attention back to the metal pot – the water was boiling over the side. Using a towel to protect her hands, she moved the pot to the edge of the fire.

A voice came from the darkness. 'Dinner ready?'

'Francis?'

Francis walked into the firelight. 'Sorry I was gone a while. Hope you weren't worried.'

'I was – where have you been?' Lucy realised she sounded like her mother. 'I was *really* worried.'

'I went visiting,' Francis smiled mischievously. 'And I've brought a friend to dinner.' He turned and gave a couple of low, reassuring squeaks. A smaller pig, a sow about the same age as Francis, stepped uneasily towards Lucy.

'This is Celia,' Francis said shyly. 'I caught a whiff of a pig farm this morning and I went exploring.'

'That must be Joe Lee's place. At Winna Creek. He knows Uncle Reg.'

'It wasn't far and, well, I met Celia there.' At the mention of her name, Celia moved closer to the fire and sniffed at Lucy's arm.

She reached out and tickled the sow behind the ear. 'She seems very friendly.'

'I'm pleased you like her,' said Francis. 'I thought maybe it was time I had a girlfriend.'

'Francis, this is hardly the time for a romance. Besides you're only –'

'I'm a fully grown pig,' Francis stated flatly. 'And she's a fully grown sow.'

Lucy knew he was right and, anyway, she was glad he was back. 'You want that spaghetti now?'

'You betcha – totally unreal! Yes!' Francis enthused. 'I told Celia about it and she wants some too.' He squeaked a few sounds and Celia joined in enthusiastically.

'OK, cut the racket,' Lucy said. 'Do you guys like orange cordial as well?'

The fire burnt low and hot and Lucy stirred the red coals with a stick thoughtfully. Francis sat on his hind legs and looked over the sea at the bright stars. Celia lay by his side, asleep, snoring gently.

'The stars are beautiful, aren't they?' Francis said after a long silence. 'I never knew they'd sparkle so brilliantly.'

'It's a great night.' Lucy lifted her arm to point. 'That's the Southern Cross.'

'I wonder if it's fine in Elsewhere tonight.'

'Elsewhere? Where do you mean exactly?' Lucy asked.

'I've heard about it on the radio. Dr Price has it on in her office sometimes, and I hear the weather forecast. They always say "Elsewhere it will be fine",' Francis said. 'Weather's always good there apparently.'

Lucy laughed. 'That's silly ... elsewhere just means other places on the weather map. Not here.'

'Oh, I often wondered about that. Not here ... oh, right.'

Lucy broke a flaming coal with the stick and

watched the fire flare up. 'Francis, I don't know what to do now. I'm not sure how long we can hide.'

'I've been thinking about that too.'

'All I know is that I don't want them to get you,' Lucy said. 'I won't let them do anything to you.' Francis shuffled closer and Lucy leant her head against his shoulder.

'Perhaps it'd be easier if I decided,' he said. 'After all, I'm an intelligent being, I have a human brain.'

'I've still got some money.' Lucy felt the change and notes in her pocket. 'We could take a bus and keep hiding in other places, if we have to. And Uncle Reg would help us out.'

'It couldn't go on very long. Eventually, they'd find us. And your parents would worry about you.'

'I don't want Dr Price and her husband to operate on you, Francis.' Lucy shuddered.

'But it is my choice, isn't it?'

'They'll kill you.'

'They'll kill part of me – my body.'

'If the operation doesn't work, all of you will die.' Lucy stared unhappily into his eyes and saw a reflection of the stars above. And something else. 'You've already decided, haven't you?'

Francis paused to get the words right. 'Lucy, I've worked out why I'm alive. Dr Price created me, and part of my genetic material, part of my body, is Henry's.' He went quiet for a moment. 'And he's only a little boy, a boy who's never had a chance to live.'

'But what about you?'

'My brain will live on,' Francis reasoned. 'I'm different, Lucy, I'm a freak. I'll never be happy the way I am. And the pig part of my body will live only another few years. And Henry has a whole life ahead of him – fifty, maybe sixty years or more.'

'Dr Price doesn't care about you. You're just an experiment!' Lucy protested.

'I owe Henry something. For the pleasure I've had in reading and thinking about things,' Francis replied. 'And seeing the stars. And eating spaghetti alla funghi.'

Lucy leant against him and sighed.

'My brain is something I can freely give,' Francis stated. 'Honestly, I wouldn't do it for anyone else. And I should thank Dr Price for something else too.'

'What?'

'Without her, I would never have met you.' He rubbed his cheek against hers gently. 'The only friend I've ever had.'

Lucy stared into the glowing fire and fought back her tears.

Celia stirred in her sleep and gave a soft squeal. Lucy sniffed to clear her nose. 'Celia has floppy ears, you know.'

'I know, she's a Landrace. I thought I should widen the gene pool a bit.'

'What's that supposed to mean?'

'You'll find out.' Francis looked at her imploringly. 'You will look after her, won't you?'

'Yes. If that's what you want.'

'It would make me happy.'

Lucy looked directly at Francis and stroked his snout. 'Is this really what you want to do, Francis? This transplant. Have you really made up your mind?'

'Yes.'

'Then I better ring Uncle Reg.' Lucy rose. 'We'll need his help.'

24

IN THE DARK

In the dark living room, Celia snorted with surprise as Lucy trod on her right trotter.

'Sorry, Celia,' she said. 'Hey, Francis, wake up. There's someone outside.'

'Ummmmnnh?'

'Francis, lift them lids.' She tugged at his leg to wake him up. 'There's someone out there.'

'Some ... one ... who?' Francis asked sleepily.

'Look!' She whispered through her teeth. A torchbeam wobbled through a patch of scrub outside the living room window. 'Someone's coming.'

'Isn't Uncle Reg picking us up?' Francis slid off the couch and Celia got to her feet.

'Yes, but we're not meeting him until five o'clock.' Lucy moved towards the window and checked her watch. 'That's two hours away. He wouldn't get here this early.'

She tried to make out the identity of the people moving through the trees. The flash of a torchbeam revealed a distinctive cap on someone's head. 'It's the police!' she gasped. 'We'll have to escape through the garage.'

Lucy moved swiftly to the internal door that connected to the garage, opened it and let Celia and Francis trot through. 'The door's open. We'll go round the side and across the sand dunes.'

'Surround the house!' A voice called in the distance.

'Break down the door if you have to!'

Lucy recognised the familiar roar of Brian Martin's voice.

Outside, Celia and Francis made their way up the first dune. Twenty metres behind, Lucy scrambled up the first section of sandy slope and looked back. A torchbeam shone out through the garage door. 'They're inside!'

'Forget them, Lucy, come on!' Francis cried from the top of the dune.

The sand was loose and slippery and Lucy struggled in the deep steps left by the pigs. Soon, she was over the crest and racing down the other side. Francis and Celia were halfway up the next hill.

'Keep going!' Lucy urged. 'Only two more to go!' She could hear voices in the distance, but didn't dare glance back. Five minutes later, they rested on the high cliff overlooking the darkened town of Shelly Beach. Only a few street lights were on.

'Where do we go now?' Francis asked.

'Just over there.' Lucy pointed to a spot behind a pile of granite boulders. 'There's a cave – I've played there in the holidays. We'll rest for a while.'

There was a rosy hint of sunrise on the horizon as Lucy looked out of the cave entrance. Francis came alongside and sniffed the air. 'Might rain later.'

'Here – or in Elsewhere?' Lucy quipped.

Francis crinkled his lips in a smile. 'Here. I can smell it. That's why I have such a big nose.'

'That smile of yours has really come on,' Lucy said fondly.

'Had a good teacher. Do we have to go far?'

'No. And we better get moving.'

Lucy led them across the sandhills, further inland from the house. 'The old boat jetty's down in the other bay,' she explained, as they trudged through the sand.

Francis stopped in his tracks. 'I can hear someone.'

'Must be on the roadway,' Lucy answered. Ahead, trees and shrubs lined the main road into town. They'd have to cross it to get to the fisherman's hut and jetty on the other side.

Lucy tried to avoid stepping on the twigs and branches underfoot. A hundred metres away, a policeman stood by his car, pouring a hot drink from a thermos into the plastic lid. He took a sip, lowered his head and sat back in the car.

'Come on!' Lucy kept her eye on the policeman's back as she followed Celia and Francis across the road.

'Take it easy going down,' she whispered. The rocky path was strewn with loose stones and was hard going. It was getting lighter when they reached the beach and the dilapidated wooden jetty. Lucy's watch showed five past five.

'What do we do now?' Francis asked.

'We wait,' Lucy answered anxiously. Where was Uncle Reg?

Celia squeaked softly to Francis and his ears twitched. 'Out there. Something's coming.'

In a few seconds, Lucy heard it too, the soft put-put of an engine. A small fishing boat appeared around the point of the bay and Reg and Vittoria waved.

'There they are! Onto the jetty – quick!'

Their feet clattered on the boards as they ran along the jetty.

Reg steered towards them and brought the boat alongside.

'Morning. Care to come aboard?'

'Hurry up!' Vittoria urged. 'And I've brought some breakfast along.'

Above them, a series of blinding lights switched on along the cliff top. Brian Martin's voice boomed out of a megaphone. 'That's far enough! Stay there and no-one will get hurt!'

Celia squealed with fright, and they looked up to see Brian and a line of policemen holding powerful searchlights.

'It's a trap,' Lucy croaked.

Four policemen, led by Brian, jogged down the path towards them.

'You're all under arrest. Stay there!' a policeman called out.

'Lucy, Francis ... and ...' Reg didn't know the sow's name.

'Celia,' Lucy said.

'When I count to three – jump into the boat. We'll make a dash for it ... Ready?'

'Ready ...' Lucy balanced on her toes.

'1 ... 2 ... 3!' Reg revved the engine till it screamed, and Francis immediately pushed Celia into the boat. 'Uggh!' Vittoria grunted as she caught the sow and they collapsed in a heap.

'Don't let them get away!' Brian's voice boomed in the still morning air.

'Go, Francis, go!' Lucy cried.

Francis gathered his strength and leapt into the bow of the boat.

'Lucy, Lucy!' Reg urged from the wheel.

The boat moved out from the jetty and she jumped in beside Francis. 'Step on it, Uncle Reg. Step on it!'

Brian's big feet and bulky body pounded down the jetty, and with a last desperate lunge, he dived at the stern of the boat. He belly-flopped and a huge column of water splashed over Lucy and Francis.

'Thanks a lot!' Lucy called back.

'See ya, ya dirty rat!' Francis yelled.

Brian's head bobbed up above the surface. 'I'll get you, Reg,' he gurgled. 'I'll get you for this!'

With a smile of satisfaction, Reg pushed the boat to full power and the jetty quickly disappeared behind them.

'Where's that food?' Francis asked. 'I'm starving.'

Reg and Vittoria looked at him with a shocked expression. Reg spoke first. 'Did he ...?'

'He eats anything,' Lucy said. 'Feed him or he'll never shut up.'

25
THE TWIST

In the back of the truck, Matilda and Celia rubbed their necks against Francis and generally made a fuss of him.

'You don't mind me bringing them?' Francis asked Lucy.

'I'm glad they're here,' she replied quietly, as the truck slowed in the laneway behind the headquarters of the Genius Genes Corporation. It was after eight o'clock, and although they'd passed through heavy city traffic, the narrow street was deserted.

Reg tooted the horn. A rear door opened in the building and Amanda came out.

Francis sniffed around Celia's ears, gave her

a fond lick and paused to look at Matilda. 'Nice meeting you, Mother,' he squeaked. 'Stay well.'

'Goodbye, Son.' Matilda gave him the traditional pig farewell. 'Go to where the good pigs go.'

Reg put the plank in place and Francis smiled gratefully as he stepped down to the roadway.

'Great smile,' Reg said to Lucy. 'I'll leave you two for a minute.'

Lucy knelt in front of Francis and wrapped her arms around his neck. 'I don't want you to go.'

'At the end, when Oliver Twist went to see Fagin in prison, he said "I am not afraid". I'm not afraid either, Lucy,' Francis said. 'Don't worry.'

'I didn't know it till last night, but you've been a good friend to me too,' she said emotionally. 'The best friend I've ever had.'

'You've got lots of friends.'

'Not like you.' Lucy wiped the tears from her eyes. 'I love you, Francis.'

'And I love you too.' He put his left trotter around her shoulder. 'My friend.'

Francis noticed Amanda standing by the

door. She looked tired and worried and he felt sorry for her. 'I better go now,' he said. 'Catch ya later.'

He licked a tear from Lucy's cheek and stepped away from her.

'Bye ... piggy.'

Francis gave the biggest smile he could manage.

'Bye ... dag.'

26
A WAKE-UP CALL

Lucy hitched the heavy bag onto her shoulder and walked through the elevator doors. At the ward reception desk, Dr Price was talking to one of the nurses.

'Hi, Dr Price,' Lucy said. 'Can I go in and see him?'

'Yes, of course, Lucy,' she replied. 'But don't expect too much. He only woke up this morning.'

'Is he OK?'

'Well, coming out of a two-month coma is difficult for anyone. But all the signs are good.'

Lucy found the room and walked quietly inside. A thin figure lay under a sheet, with his back to the door. She tiptoed to the bed and touched him on the shoulder. 'Francis, Francis – can you hear me?'

For half a minute there was no reaction. Lucy squeezed his hand. 'Francis, are you awake?'

The boy turned over slowly, his eyes opened and he smiled. 'Hi. I think you better call me Henry now.'

'Right, you look exactly the same. How are you feeling?'

'Can't get used to scratching my nose with my fingers. And I feel like an apple, a big, juicy Granny Smith.'

'No apples, I'm afraid, but I did bring something else.'

'Bananas or pears – I don't mind.'

'Better than that. A real surprise.' Lucy swung the bag from her shoulder, reached in and a tiny, pink piglet wriggled in her hands. 'You're a father. Congratulations!'

'Is Celia OK?'

'Yes. She's at Uncle Reg's farm.'

'Is he like ... like me?'

As Lucy passed the piglet to him, it started to cry. The sound echoed through the room and out into the corridor. The cry of a human baby.

'What do you want to call him?' Lucy asked.

'Roger,' he said. 'Roger Bacon.'

VIVIEN ALCOCK

The Monster Garden

'I shouldn't have done it. I didn't really mean to, but that's no excuse, of course. I should have known better with a name like mine. Frances Stein. Called Frankie for short. You can't really blame me for making a monster . . .'

The day she acquired some living tissue from the genetic engineering laboratory was the day Frankie's life changed for ever. She'd never imagined her experiment would be so successful, but how will she keep the growing monster a secret from her family?

The Monster Garden was shortlisted for the Smarties, Whitbread, Guardian and Federation of Children's Book Groups Awards, and was commended for the Carnegie Medal.

GILLIAN CROSS

Crazy Shoe Shuffle

It is Lee's worst day ever! First, sour Mr Merton confiscates his football. Secondly, Lee makes sweet Miss Cherry cross. Thirdly, bossy Mrs Puddock, the headmistress, forces him to eat his disgusting school dinner.

On top of it all, he finds himself sorting out the shoe mountain in the cloakroom for Miss Cherry and gets on the wrong side of Mr Merton and Mrs Puddock again!

But on the way home he meets a strange old woman and suddenly the boot is on the other foot. The three teachers find themselves in the children's shoes and they're right out of step with everyone else. Only Lee knows what's happened – and he'll have to keep on his toes if he wants to save them from falling flat on their faces . . .

ANNE FINE

The Granny Project

Shortlisted for the Guardian Children's Fiction Award.

To the four children, Ivan, Sophie, Tanya and Nicholas, Granny is a bit of a dotty old lady – sometimes demanding, sometimes a nuisance, and often annoying – but as much a part of their lives as the shambly house or the whirring washing machine. How could their mother and father decide to put her in a home?

'Anne Fine writes with wit and ingenuity, her characters are lively and the dialogue sparkles . . . a remarkable story which illumines a common family problem with sympathy, wisdom and a great deal of humour.'
Lance Salway, *Signal*

'a genuinely funny family novel which incorporates uncomfortable truths about physical and mental deterioration with a spiky, unsentimental style . . .'
British Book News

JENNY NIMMO

Delilah and the Dogspell

Delilah, huge, fluffy grey, wide golden-eyed, is a cat who is more than she seems. Delilah specialises in dogspells. When dogs start shrinking, Annie steps in. But Annie has a soft spot for Delilah . . .

A fast-moving fantasy by the prize-winning author of *The Snow Spider*.

'a most attractive read . . . The book is a romp, splendidly done, and must be a delightful choice . . .'
School Librarian

CHRIS POWLING

Famous with Smokey Joe

He pulled the goggles over his face.

At once the world went golden: golden close up, golden far off and golden in-between, as if a mad King Midas had been out on a tickling spree. 'Keep your eyes set on the carborundum,' ordered Smokey Joe. 'Feel the edge of the blade through your fingertips.'

Zac is a city boy who can't imagine the country has anything of interest for him until he meets Smokey Joe, an eccentric old knife-grinder who asks Zac to join him on his travels. Together they begin a magical and meaningful journey.

CARA LOCKHART SMITH

Pzazz!

When their parents win a holiday to Mexico, Jane and her brother Wolfie are whisked off to stay with their magician uncle, Mr Sol Dodds. But he is in a deep, deep sleep. In charge of the house is Skvattsky the Remarkable I.Q. cat. But even more remarkable is the mysterious Pzazz. When Wolfie opens the Pzazz jar, magic spills out . . .

A very funny, touching and energetic story by the award-winning author of *Parchment House* and *Dudley Shadow*, described by *Books for Keeps* as 'a quick and unusual read.'

ROBERT WESTALL

The Night Mare

Miss Crimond was sitting in Dad's chair which had once been Grandpa's chair; and Billy hated her.

To Billy and all the families who rented her houses in Back Tennyson Street, Miss Crimond was the arch enemy.

Billy and his gang declare war. In between the street cricket and football, they go into battle. There is the firework down the chimney that fills the house with soot; the deliveries, not requested by Miss Crimond, of coal she has to pay for and manure that comes up to her eyes.

But Billy's campaign has unexpected consequences when he sees the night mare, the horse of his dreams, and finds out what a special and clever man his grandpa had been . . .

y effort is made to keep prices low, it is sometimes necessary to increase prices at short notice .
Paperbacks reserves the right to show new retail prices on covers which may differ from those
previously advertised in the text or elsewhere.

The prices shown below were correct at the time of going to press.

☐	7497 2646 6	**The Face at the Window**	Vivien Alcock	£3.99
☐	7497 2067 0	**The Parsley Parcel**	Elizabeth Arnold	£3.99
☐	7497 2388 2	**Whispers in the Graveyard**	Theresa Breslin	£3.99
☐	7497 1794 7	**Born of the Sun**	Gillian Cross	£3.99
☐	7497 1066 7	**The Animals of Farthing Wood**	Colin Dann	£3.99
☐	7497 1823 4	**White Peak Farm**	Berlie Doherty	£3.50
☐	7497 0184 6	**The Summer House Loon**	Anne Fine	£3.99
☐	7497 0962 6	**The Away Team**	Michael Hardcastle	£2.99
☐	7497 0136 6	**I Am David**	Anne Holm	£3.99
☐	7497 1664 9	**Hiding Out**	Elizabeth Laird	£4.50
☐	7497 0791 7	**The Ghost of Thomas Kempe**	Penelope Lively	£3.99
☐	7497 2644 X	**The Voices of Silence**	Bel Mooney	£3.99
☐	7497 1754 8	**The War of Jenkins' Ear**	Michael Morpurgo	£3.99
☐	7497 0831 X	**The Snow Spider**	Jenny Nimmo	£3.99
☐	7497 0656 2	**Journey of 1000 Miles**	Ian Strachan	£3.99
☐	7497 2734 9	**Panther in Argyll**	Lisa Tuttle	£3.99
☐	7497 0796 8	**Kingdom by the Sea**	Robert Westall	£3.99

All these books are available at your bookshop or newsagent, or can be ordered direct from the address
below. Just tick the titles you want and fill in the form below.

Cash Sales Department, PO Box 5, Rushden, Northants NN10 6YX.
Fax: 01933 414047 : Phone: 01933 414000.

Please send cheque, payable to 'Reed Book Services Ltd.', or postal order for purchase price quoted and
allow the following for postage and packing:

£1.00 for the first book, 50p for the second; **FREE POSTAGE AND PACKING FOR THREE BOOKS OR MORE
PER ORDER.**

NAME (Block letters) ....

ADDRESS...

....

☐ I enclose my remittance for...........................

☐ I wish to pay by Access/Visa Card Number ☐☐☐☐☐☐☐☐☐☐☐☐☐☐

Expiry Date ☐☐☐☐

Signature . . . .

Please quote our reference: MAND